CODY'S RETURN

THE JUSTICE TRILOGY BOOK ONE

STEPHEN MERTZ

ROUGH
EDGES
PRESS

Cody's Return
Paperback Edition
© Copyright 2022 Stephen Mertz

Rough Edges Press
An Imprint of Wolfpack Publishing
5130 S. Fort Apache Rd. 215-380
Las Vegas, NV 89148

roughedgespress.com

Paperback ISBN 978-1-68549-061-4
LCCN 2022930241

CODY'S RETURN

CHAPTER ONE

GREB VETROV BRACED against the violent lurch as the train began moving.

The 21st Century diesel locomotive's twelve hundred horsepower exerted tremendous force breaking inertia, sending a clanking groan rippling along the length of freight cars like some giant creature of iron flexing its two million pounds of muscle. The platform markings provided a gauge of the train's acceleration, the markings crawling past slowly at first but soon flashing by and out of Vetrov's peripheral vision.

No one was present on the platform to witness the train's departure or to observe its cargo: a half-dozen nuclear warheads bound for North Korea.

At fifty-three, Vetrov had the deeply lined, stoic features of his Russian and Ukrainian peasant heritage. Stocky and in good physical shape, he was average in appearance, something that had always worked to his advantage given the relentless ambition he'd been born with. To the best of his knowledge, no photograph of him had been made public in years. This allowed him considerable freedom of international movement.

He clutched the railing in the locomotive where he stood near the controls and the engine crew. He tried to ignore the thoughts of possible rip-offs and betrayal that preyed on his mind despite the fortune in bribes paid and all of the high-level precautions in play.

The crew on this trip included a team of his personal security force, veteran Spetsnaz commandos, highly trained, proficient solders, once the cream of Soviet Special Forces who'd honed their skills in wars in the Georgian Republic and the decades-long North Caucasus insurgency, as well as moonlighting for the Russian mafia. They rode this train not because he expected trouble from the authorities but, rather, to ensure that none of his competitors had designs on hijacking these nukes. Not that there was any real chance of that happening. The simple fact, however, was that there were few if any who equaled Greb Vetrov's reputation as *the* global arms dealer specializing in the sale of diverted Soviet-era Russian nukes.

He took considerable pride in being the most wanted man in Russia, sought by Russian authorities and law enforcement agencies throughout the world. He'd come a long way since his earliest days operating a combine harvester as a youth on a collective farm. By the time he retired from the Russian army as a noted military strategist who literally wrote the book on prevailing nuclear endgame theory, he had risen through the ranks to reach the autonomous position of overseeing his country's entire tactical nuclear arsenal.

The only aircraft he anticipated seeing was the attack helicopter on its way to escort this shipment in case the North Koreans decided to try a double-cross. The chopper had been requisitioned through deep cover connections Vetrov maintained within the military. The aircraft's 30mm auto-cannon and anti-personnel missiles would be more than enough should the North Koreans try anything dirty.

The train's speed was rapidly approaching its peak. The Soviet-era military base fell away behind them. The morning sky was a clear blue, not a cloud in sight, the air retaining the crisp, nippy chill of the night. Winter lasts longer than summer throughout the Urals.

For more than a year prior to his retirement, Vetrov had gone about quietly recruiting and organizing a small paramilitary force. A private army, according to an accurate Interpol assessment. And with the help of a very few highly placed co-conspirators serving positions of authority in the government and military, he had undertaken the audacious crime of diverting a stockpile of nukes that were now stored in this remote, long-deserted military rail facility in the high country of the Ural Mountains in eastern Russia. Six months after his retirement from the Army, Vetrov began selling off from that stockpile to terrorist groups and rogue nations.

North Korea promised a massive payday and Vetrov had seen evidence of this in the huge amount of their down payment on these nukes. But that meant little. A nation as hard-strapped, with as few resources, as North Korea could well prefer gaining the nukes without paying for them, saving them the purchase price balance of millions and gaining enough firepower to wipe out just about anyone.

When the military locomotive reached top speed it would be unstoppable by anything short of a tank shell or a bombing run. Trained gunmen, himself included, would be a deterrent to a primitive hi-jacking attempt but a 30mm auto-cannon and anti-personnel missiles would be the punishment facing any such attempt by Pyongyang. Unless the North Koreans expected to nearly set off World War III here and now by sending a warship, the gunship would obliterate whatever bathtub toy was sent to confront him.

Vetrov paused in thought for a moment, taken in as always by the unending panorama of majestic high country through which the train travelled. He was not easily intimidated but even aboard this powerful, driving locomotive, one felt dwarfed by the surrounding natural sights.

Rising along the eastern edge of the Russian plain, the north-south spine of the Urals extends 1300 miles from the Arctic coast to the border with Kazakhstan, forming the natural traditional boundary between Europe and Asia. The great mineral resources of Russia are in the Urals. Iron ore is mined in the south along with rich deposits of coal and copper while these northern regions were remote and mostly undeveloped. The train's route would follow and track through low passes, both natural and those cut through a rugged terrain of summits generally between 4000 and 6000 feet.

Dead reckoning had them at the coast in a little over six hours.

Butenko, the commander of Vetrov's security team, entered the cabin from a back section of the locomotive. A bearded giant of a man, he wore a MAC-10 compact machine pistol/submachine gun hanging on a sling about his neck.

"Sir, there's a truck coming up on us."

Vetrov looked back to see a high plume of dust spewing angrily into the air, advancing along the graveled roadbed of train tracks. A Toyota pickup truck, of all things, with a man crouching in its bed, poised to make a wild leap once the truck could get him close enough for a jump.

Vetrov cursed.

Preparations had been made for hijackers and law enforcement, yes, but this was something else. He always carefully monitored his backtrack and recently had picked up a number of indications that someone—no one reporting to him was exactly sure who—had been probing, investigating, tracking and closing in on this operation in subtle but detectable ways. Vetrov's gut told him he was looking at the "who" in question. A commando agent of some sort, no doubt, and he had to be the best to have gotten this close.

Butenko seemed to read his mind.

"It's got to be him," he growled. "The one who's been tracking us."

"We have to stop him immediately," said Vetrov. "I'll get the train to speed up. Get your men after him."

Butenko's response was to hurry from the cabin.

Vetrov brought up his binoculars to scan the length of the train just in time to see the man in the pickup truck make his death-defying leap.

CHAPTER TWO

JACK CODY SNATCHED the bottom rung of the speeding freight car ladder.

Automatic gunfire ripped the air, raining down on him and the speeding Toyota pickup truck from which he'd jumped.

The train, blistering along now at just short of eighty miles an hour, shook and rattled, a quarter mile-long serpentine bronco seeking to hurl Cody against the gravel flying by underneath or, worse, between the unyielding steel rails and wheels. If that happened, thousands of tons of locomotive and cars would dice him into stew meat within seconds.

Cody was in peak athletic physical condition but fighting the train's jolting centrifugal force to climb the freight car's utility ladder required Herculean effort. Without a hold for leverage, his boots were suspended dangerously close to the ground as he forcefully pulled himself up, all upper body strength with tendons quivering and straining.

Behind him the pickup was swerving away hard,

disappearing in a cloud of dust, gravel . . . and a loud crash.

Cody's gut tightened. There was nothing he could do for the driver, Tanya Lubyanka. They were miles from the closest habitation and even that was only the seemingly run-down Russian base Vetrov had overhauled for storage of his diverted nuclear warheads. If Tanya was injured, there was no medical help available. The sound of a sudden crash could have merely been her truck hitting a rut or rocks, survivable. But there was nothing Cody could do about that now.

Twelve nuclear weapons, one on the very freight car he clung to, were on their way to dangerous hands. He wasn't afraid of death but he *did* fear the deadly payload aboard this train and the consequences of its delivery to North Korea.

Drawing himself up far enough to hook his feet on the bottom rung of the ladder, with four points of contact with the steps he managed to reach the top rung. Glancing over the top of the freight car, he spotted two of Vetrov's Russian gangsters with MAC-10s advancing precariously atop a container a few cars down. A short, lightweight SMG, the MAC-10 is chambered for .45 rounds in a 30-round magazine; a highly accurate weapon for short-range outdoor action.

Still clutching the ladder's top rung, Cody lowered his head. He shifted each foot to the narrow ledge along the bottom of the car, hanging on by the car's grab irons. The wind was blowing hard over the rumble of the big iron wheels just below him.

But they'd seen him! Another burst of auto fire. Ricochets spanged off the edge of the roof where Cody had been moments earlier.

He hooked one arm around the ladder, his free hand

unleathering his Beretta from its shoulder rig. With the ground a speeding blur close beneath him, he tugged a thin cord attached to the holster and clipped it on the metal lanyard loop of the pistol. If he lost his grip on it, he wouldn't lose the Beretta thanks to the cord connected to his body. He needed to make his way up front to the locomotive but doing so made him an easy target. He straightened to his full height, head and shoulders barely visible over the freight car's roof so as to present a small target.

The gunmen didn't see him at first, each man concentrating on reloading his weapon as they advanced in a low crab walk along the rooftops.

Cody snapped off a round that caught one gunman in the shin, shattering bone and pitching him off the train with a scream of terror that ended abruptly when he hit the ground and bounced under the train's grinding wheels.

The second Russian threw himself flat, firing a burst on full auto. A bullet snapped close to Cody's head but the MAC-10's recoil and the violent motion of the barreling train sent the rest of the slugs whining high over him.

Cody fired twice. That ended the MAC-10's chatter. He then used both hands to climb atop the train car. As he made it atop, the Beretta on its lanyard bounced against his shin. He reeled it back into his hand, advancing along the shuddering freight car.

Atop the next car, the body of the Russian gunman lay motionless. Cody prepared to take a leap across the gap between the cars when he spotted a detail about the "dead" guy. The Russian lay on the next car with one hand folded beneath him, the other hand white knuckled around a rung to maintain his place as the train negotiated mountainous twists and turns. Sensing Cody's hesitation, he suddenly went from playing possum to rolling over with an ugly snarl, tracking a handgun in Cody's direction. He got off one shot that missed by inches because Cody arched sideways.

Cody triggered a round that struck true. The Russian's white knuckles lost their grip. His lifeless form was whisked off the nearly flying train.

Cody leapt and landed on that car. He kept his feet spaced and his knees loose, flexing with each rock and wobble of the train's downhill momentum. He could not afford to slip, so with each stride he took he put his faith in his agility, his leverage and in the waffle tread of his combat boots. This wasn't the first train he'd ever surfed atop. But yeah, this time was *way* different. This time the stakes were high as they could be.

His falling off this train meant twelve cities would disappear beneath a nuclear fireball!

He advanced along the top of the train as quickly as he dared, the Beretta locked tight in his fist, his eyes sharp in anticipation of other gunmen. Greb Vetrov would hardly have only two gunmen to protect this payload of mega death.

A man appeared from between two cars up ahead. Cody threw himself flat. Rippling pops filled the air inches above him with sizzling lead. He returned fire with two rounds. The enemy fire ceased. But that didn't mean the man was down.

Cody scrambled to the next gap between two of the wildly rocking train cars where he flung himself through the air to catch hold of the next car's ladder, keeping down to the blind spot. Angry projectiles resumed buzzing just above him. He clutched the ladder's top rung with both hands, the Beretta secured to his shoulder holster by its length of paracord. He chanced a quick look around the side of the freight car.

Three men were advancing along this side of the freight car, using its utility handholds. Having decided that advancing via the top of the train was too treacherous, they'd cinched their MAC-10s over their shoulders by slings. They were advancing rapidly. A fourth man, standing on a ladder between this car and the next, was providing them with cover fire.

It was a two-pronged assault that left no safe route to Cody's goal: the locomotive. Tanya's initial approach had intended to set him up for a leap from the Toyota onto the locomotive but when auto fire greeted the truck, it hadn't worked out that way and here he was, pinned down.

"*No*," Cody growled to himself, "*it does not end here!*"

He drew the Beretta up on its lanyard and holstered the pistol, needing both hands for his surge up the ladder. Retreat was not an option. Not with this much at stake. He broke into a run across the top of the freight car.

He was not unaware of the fact that he'd picked up a nickname over the course of his recent missions for the CIA. He only accepted what were classified as suicide missions. He had his reasons and the moniker stuck. They called him Suicide Cody. Dying on a suicide mission, yeah, maybe that was suicide like they said. But when his number came up, Cody intended to go out kicking ass.

Another car length ahead was the gunman mounted on the ladder. This one brought up his weapon with only a hint of panic on his face at sight of the crazy man storming directly at him, making a perfect target. He opened fire. The overhang lip of the freight car's roof caught the initial burst. Sparks danced wildly.

Cody kept coming.

The Russian lifted his weapon's muzzle with his human target practically upon him. But he wasn't fast enough. Cody sprung across the gap with a single bound, dropping a hip, his combat boots striking out straight before him. Their waffle tread landed hard on the guy's face. The crunch of facial bone rippled through the soles, followed by the man being swept off the train as if by a giant invisible hand.

Cody gripped the ladder's top rung and hoisted himself onto the freight car's roof. Drawing the Beretta M9, he stretched out to glance over the side, down on this trio of hardened Russian soldiers who'd sold out to work for a global arms dealer. Their faces were etched with the effort of making their way along the side of the hurtling train which was now hammering its way across an ancient trestle far above the rugged terrain. A tumble now would be fatal for anyone involved.

The closest Russian hardcase suddenly lunged up to wrap vise-like fingers around Cody's wrist. An iron grip. Cody grunted at the sudden pull, his handhold shifting as if nails were driven through his grasping hand. He and the Russian were locked together, each with one hand on the train, their weight and strength canceling each other's effort, the aggressive attack making it impossible for Cody to pull off a shot with the Beretta or kick. Any such forcible shift in his weight would break his grip on the handhold and over he'd go.

The brawny gunman managed to wrap both his hands around Cody's forearm, somehow managed to swing his considerable heft onto the roof. Cody brought up a blob of mucus and spat it directly into the man's eye. Wasted spit. The guy's iron-spring grip didn't loosen. Cody's next move, committed in the adrenaline-driven survival mode of the moment, would definitely have been considered suicidal by any rational person. He released his grip of the handhold on the roof's lip.

This sent both men jolting lengthwise along the freight car's roof. Centrifugal force of the highballing train forced the bleary-eyed Russian to release his hold on Cody's forearm, the guy clawing frantically for another handhold. Cody grasped at the same handhold with both of his hands. Arresting his own tumble, he put all of his strength into a double-knee kick into his opponent's rib cage and armpit. The blow's effect was twofold. The knee to the ribs emptied the man's lungs while the kick to his armpit numbed his arm. In an instant, he was breathless, dangling over the edge by only his fingers.

Cody stabbed out with another kick, this time with enough range of motion to deliver a hammer-like blow to the jaw. Cody's boots had steel toe caps. The guy's grip on the handhold loosened then gave way, his eyes glazed by the disruption of the blood supply to his brain. The kick either killed or rendered him unconscious because his body hurtled off the train and out of sight beyond and below the receding trestle.

The remaining pair of men was continuing along the side of the rattling train, coming toward Cody, their faces set with their effort and determination. Another made it onto the roof, bringing his MAC-10 off his shoulder and around. Cody nailed him with a head shot. The guy shuddered, stumbling three steps to the side and over he went, another dead man brushed from the train.

The last of this team poked his head out over the roof of the rocking and rolling freight car. This one came prepared, his MAC-10 held at the low ready, but that did him no good. Cody drilled his face with a single bullet and the guy was gone.

Drawing a deep breath, Cody released his grip on the handhold. Steadying himself on one knee, allowing himself to gain a semblance of his own balance, he granted himself the luxury of taking several deep breaths to recharge the inner man while palming a fresh magazine into the Beretta. He was about to resume his approach of the locomotive when a premonition brought his attention around just in time to see a burly, bearded Russian coming at his blind side, the clattering of train noise having concealed his approach.

Butenko had acquired a short-handled military entrenching tool—a compact shovel—and was swinging it at Cody's head.

Cody blocked the down-swing with his left forearm, reaching his right hand across to grasp the shovel handle. The block angled the blade away from slicing him, staggering the big Russian bear who had a hundred pounds on Cody and at least eighteen inches in height. In his effort to regain hold of the shovel, the guy followed through and somehow got hold of Cody, lifting him over his head with one mighty snarl and then slamming Cody down onto unyielding metal.

Cody's breath exploded from his lungs. He couldn't make out Butenko's scowling words over the blood rushing in his ears and the clatter of the train underneath him. The Russian moved in, swinging at the prone Cody with both hands as if he held a battle axe. Cody rolled, feeling the burning sparks of metal on metal sting the back of his neck. The Russian grunted and staggered back, out of reach of any counter attack. Cody assumed a four point stance, elbows and knees flexed for instant movement.

He wished he had something to counter the shovel in this guy's hands. His Beretta dangled at the end of its coiled cord. If he tried to palm the grip, the Russian would be atop him in no time. Instead, he jerked up the lanyard cord, not reeling the pistol into his hand but whipping the two-and-a-half-pound handgun around his head once like a flail. The pistol's cord wrapped around Butenko's forearm, tangling around the limb. Cody yanked hard on the semi-elastic cord, breaking the guy's two-handed hold on the damn shovel.

This did not deter the Russian. He closed in again, raising the shovel back high to deliver a skull-crushing blow. But even as the shovel cocked back, Cody lanced a kick into the man's side, just above his hip, the steel-toed boot punching the kidney. An explosion of agony made the big man shudder. His knees knocked. The shovel lowered.

Cody pulled on the lanyard cord that was wrapped about the man's arm, yanking him in closer and delivering a hard head butt to Butenko's nose. Cartilage crunched and hot bloody droplets sprayed Cody in the face.

The guy dropped to one knee but he was not down for the count. He still held the shovel. He shook his head once to clear it and then lashed out with the shovel, its razor- sharp edge slicing through the air scant inches from Cody's jugular vein.

Cody snapped his elbow up, striking hard at the bloody remains of a nose, snapping the Russian's skull back. As soon as the Adam's apple was exposed, Cody slashed down with the hard edge of his hand, resulting in the *crunch!* of the Russian's windpipe. The big bear finally let go of the shovel, his hands going to his crushed throat. Cody untangled his pistol from around the guy's arm and fired twice into his chest. Gasping, Butenko tumbled from the train.

Lowering himself to one knee, Cody allowed his breathing to slow down, taking deep inhalations and exhaling slowly for a half minute, breathing fresh energy into exhausted muscles.

Then, cutting through the rattling racket of the train, he heard a new sound.

A deep, rhythmic thumping of the atmosphere. Louder as it grew closer. A rumbling channeled through breaks in the mountainous terrain.

Helicopter!

A huge helicopter gunship rose from behind a towering rock formation. The oversized gunship was practically on top of them! The throbbing of its rotors enveloped everything, pounding at Cody's eardrums. A monstrous aircraft with an air speed of 200 mph, bristling with machine guns and tank-killing missiles. An impressive airborne beast-of-prey wrapped in armor that was capable of withstanding the heaviest anti-aircraft fire.

Greb Vetrov's ace in the hole!

Cody gritted his teeth. He turned and pressed on along the roof of the train, struggling to maintain his balance as the train raced around a nasty curve. The nonstop thumping of the helicopter's rotors drowned out everything. He leaped onto the next car, making his way onward.

He had a train to stop. Could he somehow maneuver the attack helicopter into inadvertently destroying the train?

Suicide Cody intended to find out.

CHAPTER THREE

WHEN VETROV HEARD the rumble of the helicopter, he hailed it on the radio. He'd been visually monitoring the firefight raging atop the train. Butenko, dead! A team of seasoned pros, wiped out! What manner of superman were they up against?

"Owl One, Owl One, do you read?"

"Copy, sir!" came the prompt reply. *"Who's the stowaway I see down there?"*

"Someone who needs removal. Too bad you're loaded too heavily to fire at him."

"Copy that," Owl One answered. *"Except, I do have an idea . . ."*

"As long as we're not blowing up these weapons, do it!" ordered Vetrov.

———

CODY ADVANCED along the roof of the train.

How many more men did Vetrov have aboard under his command? The sudden appearance of the combat chopper was unexpected but at least the gunship was as powerless against him as he was against it. Its windshield glass could eat 9mm bullets from his Beretta with no trouble; same for .45 rounds from a MAC-10.

The helo, with its speed and mobility advantage over the locomotive, could kill Cody from any angle. But so what? Its armament, from mini-guns to the 30mm cannon mounted under its chin, could not be used in an extreme scenario like this. The pilot, obviously prearranged to "ride shotgun" on Vetrov's train, knew that a single lucky—make that *un*lucky—hit would result in an explosion that could burst one or more of the warheads. At which point one of two things could happen. The payload might detonate, destroying the train, the helicopter and everything for miles . . . or the casing around the fissile material for the bomb could shatter, resulting in an upwind release of deadly levels of gamma ray. The man piloting glared at Cody from the bubble front cockpit, a smirk on his face.

They actually made eye contact.

The pilot laughed and gave Cody the finger. The gunship swung in close. Cody was an easy target. Would the pilot use the helo's landing gear to bump him off the train? The relative speed difference between locomotive and chopper was too great for that; one miscalculation and the giant gunship would be smashed to smithereens. The rocky terrain of low cliff walls the train was presently passing through formed an extended natural canyon whizzing by to either side of the train. The gunship's rotors needed more radius to fly close over the train.

The pilot delivered a surprise.

The sides of the chopper blazed to flaming life, firing a half-dozen flares. Tiny rockets of nearly blinding bright silver light designed as a defense against anti-aircraft missiles. The flares burned hot enough to blind the infrared sensors of a heat-seeking missile at 2000 degrees Fahrenheit. The first salvo missed Cody but came close enough, the flesh-searing heat feeling as if he'd been thrown into an open oven.

He rushed on, hoping the pilot would fall back. The salvo had burned in mid-air just ahead. Smoke from the burning flares stung Cody's eyes and nostrils as the train barreled through the choking cloud. At last he reached the final freight car, leaving only a passenger-like "crew car" that rode coupled directly behind the locomotive. Cody lowered himself down his car's ladder, preparing to make the short hop to the crew car.

The speeding train negotiated a curve and went high-balling down a grade, causing Cody to lose his balance, almost sending him flying off into the slipstream. But somehow he maintained his hold. He gained the crew car and leaned in to open its rear entrance door.

The door would not budge.

The guy leaning his weight against the door from inside to prevent its opening was visible through the glass upper half of the door. He wore an engineer's uniform, indicating that Vetrov's team had been eliminated. The train's crew was now being drafted into action. Cody threw his full weight against the door. The man inside fell away. Then Cody was inside. The crewman had been flung into the aisle of the otherwise vacant car, his arm broken. His pistol had dropped to the floor with him. Cody kicked the handgun further along a row of seats. The stunned crewman started for the gun. Two quick rounds from the Beretta put an end to that.

Holstering the Beretta, Cody picked up the handgun and briefly examined it: a current issue Russian sidearm, the Gsh-18. Examining the ammo, he saw the blue-and-white tips of the bullets; a plastic sleeve over each bullet's tip, the blue hardened variant of steel, visible through the tip of each slug.

"Armor piercing," Cody murmured.

These rounds were designed to penetrate nearly a centimeter of steel plate. It might not shatter the hull of a Russian attack helicopter but maybe it could do something against the cockpit and the pilot.

He surged on through the crew car. Exiting it, he continued with one more leap to gain a railed walkway along the side of the locomotive; the side facing the gunship. The pilot swung the chopper up, a nasty smile on his face, likely for another salvo with his flares. Cody braced himself on the metal walkway and opened fire with the Russian handgun, firing four fast rounds.

The chopper jolted, its armored glass suddenly rendered opaque by the impact of four plate-sized craters. The pilot brought the helicopter up and away, spurred by the realization that Cody now had more bite.

Cody advanced along the railed walkway toward the door that would take him into the locomotive. That door burst open when he was short paces away from it. The engineer emerged, armed with a MAC- 10. This had to be Vetrov's last line of defense! Cody almost felt sorry for the train's engineer; a captain going down with his ship. He didn't look like a combatant. But his life choices had brought him to this and one doesn't survive a firefight by showing compassion for an enemy coming at you armed with a MAC-10. Vetrov must've had an escape plan, probably involving the chopper, and this poor chump wasn't part of it. *Too bad*, thought Cody. He caught the engineer by the lapels of his coveralls and sent the guy tumbling over the railing.

A brief scream cut through the noise of train and

helicopter before the man was ground into splattering blood and body parts from beneath grinding iron wheels.

Cody entered the main engine room, the Russian pistol extended before him. Ready for anything, he started for the complicated, oversized collection of controls, aware with every step of his surroundings: front, back, sides, ahead.

But dammit, not *up!*

The son of a bitch was waiting for him. Four paces into the engine room, Vetrov dropped onto him from the narrow service shelf over the door where he'd crouched. They tumbled to the floor together. Cody recognized the enraged face from the mission file. He was nose-to-nose with GrebVetrov, and the Russian's talon-strong fingers were at his throat. He toppled backward under the attack, Vetrov kneeing him with a kick to the kidneys. Intense stabbing pain from the blow numbed Cody's right side, causing him to lose hold of the pistol.

Vetrov snarled, "You've killed every man on this train except me!"

"You're next," said Cody. "You're not an easy man to reach."

Cody jammed a rigid thumb under Vetrov's armpit, weakening the Russian's stranglehold. He followed through with an uppercut that snapped Vetrov's head back, separating his strangling hold from Cody's throat.

Vetrov reeled back. Both men regained their footing. Vetrov grunted, coming in fast. Cody dropped to the side, his nerve ends recovered from the kidney blow. He delivered a reverse elbow that caught Vetrov in the mouth. The Russian stumbled, snarling with pain and anger. Blood dribbled from his mouth. He pivoted with surprising speed for a man his age, lashing out with another kick. Cody closed in. This blow was intended to break clavicle or ribs. Cody shifted his stance again, blunting the impact. Even so, he exhaled violently, robbed of breath. The force of the chest kick sent him backward into the wide dashboard of gauges and controls.

With a shout of triumph, Vetrov turned and hurried from the engine cabin, onto the railed metal walkway. The door closed behind him.

Cody summoned the willpower to remain upright, regaining his breath with deep inhalations, shaking his head twice to clear it. The nonstop battle atop the train, fighting his way getting to this point, had seriously tapped his tank. Sure, he was in peak physical condition but he was only human.

The *whuppa!-whuppa!* noise of the helicopter's rotors and the powerful, enveloping vibrations that went with it, penetrated the rocketing locomotive. An image came to mind as clearly as a movie scene: the terrain they were traveling through had broadened enough to allow the gunship to track the train from above. At this second a rope ladder was no doubt being lowered for Vetrov to grasp, to be lifted up and away. That was Vetrov's plan.

Cody's objective remained making sure this train and its cargo did not reach its destination. He turned to consider the controls. The labels were in Cyrillic but it didn't take much to locate the throttle. The train was racing along at 130 kilometers per hour according to the speedometer. Cody gripped the throttle collective and pushed it to the limit with one thrust. The engine gauges bolted into the red, the locomotive continuing to rapidly gain a speed well above its normal limits.

The faster the train went on these old, unmaintained tracks, the faster it would derail. That was Cody's plan.

He returned to the outside walkway just in time to see the chopper lifting up and away, extracting Vetrov. The train was indeed traveling across a relatively flat stretch of the rugged terrain. Hoping like hell that he would not be sucked beneath its grinding steel wheels, Cody dived off the speeding locomotive, hitting the hard ground in a graceless somersault that brought him up against a growth of scraggly groundcover.

Freight cars went whipping past him like a sped-up movie. Within seconds the train had passed.

No more than a minute later came the shriek of rails buckling. The sudden bronco buck-up of the serpentine train cars went screeching off the track, many of the cars standing on end. The locomotive landed on its side and went into a grinding slide creating a small dust storm. The full length of cars twisted like a giant metal anaconda, writhing in its death throes before disappearing from sight over the ledge of a vast cut in the earth from which dust and the sounds of grinding ruin filled the air.

The dust was still settling around Cody who was caked and camouflaged by the dust and gravel that had been whipped up in the train's wake.

The gunship had withdrawn and was hovering within his field of vision, downrange over the crash site, Vetrov assessing his losses. The gunship's 30mm cannon and its underwing rocket launcher pods happened at the moment to be pointing directly in Cody's direction.

For tense, eternal seconds, he froze, remaining prone, hoping that he was caked in enough detritus that it would conceal him. The helicopter was equipped with laser rangefinders and narrow range telescopic television cameras, the heavy cannon linked to the pilot's eyesight through a helmet mounted target designator. If the pilot spotted Cody, the chopper's weaponry would lock on him. A squeeze of the trigger would fire high-explosive annihilation that no man could survive.

Death did not come for him. Not this time.

The chopper eventually rose higher into the sky and disappeared into the distance. Vetrov must have assumed Cody had perished in the crash.

Cody staggered to his feet, brushing and shaking the dirt and dust from his clothes and coughing the scratch of mountain dust from his lungs. He leaned against a huge rock to get his bearings. This far into the Urals on an unused railroad line, he was days of walking to anywhere.

That's when he heard the truck's honking horn. The horn of the Toyota Hilux was familiar. He squinted back down the railroad track.

Of course.

A hell of a lot had happened since Tanya Lubyanka had gotten him aboard that train of death but no more than quarter-hour or twenty minutes had elapsed. The set of wheels Tanya drove had four-wheel-drive and had been overhauled for high speed mountain performance with the emphasis on speed. The gutsy young Russian CIA asset had tracked the train from a safe distance ever since recovering from whatever mishap occurred during the transfer. And here she was.

Tanya braked to a halt near him in a swirl of dust. A ragged line of bullet holes pockmarked the Toyota's windshield. The front grill looked wobbly. The deflated airbag dangled from the steering wheel. Tanya leaned her tousled head out the window. She'd acquired a split lip and a black eye.

"Jack!"

She was in her mid-20s; a brunette firecracker with

lively, intelligent eyes. Compact and well-proportioned, Tanya Lubyanka was a free-spirited, extremely competent country girl, Ural Mountains version. Cody liked the kid, having spent the past twenty-four hours in her company since his arrival in the region. The only downside was Tanya's addiction to 1970s American disco music which played endlessly on the truck's top end sound system. Donna Summer was in heavy rotation.

Cody hoisted himself into the passenger seat. It was her truck and Tanya had more than proven herself to be one hell of a wheelman. He surveyed the visible damage she'd sustained.

"How're you doing, kid?"

"It is an exciting day," she enthused, slightly out of breath. She peered in the direction of the dust cloud settling over the train's tangled wreckage. "You took care of those bastards who tried to kill me and my truck."

He couldn't contain a chuckle at the youthful perkiness of her.

"They won't bother you anymore," he said. The chuckle evaporated. He added, "Vetrov got away."

"You will have another chance at him," she said earnestly. "The important thing is, those missiles are not going anywhere."

"Let's hope you've got enough gas to get us somewhere."

Tanya eyed the dashboard fuel gauge. "If not," she said, "by the time we run out we should be within walking distance of civilization."

She shifted the Toyota into gear and they took off down the road. The sounds and beat of *Love to Love You, Baby* thumped from the sound system.

Even Suicide Cody had come to learn that man did not live by sacrifice and special ops alone. Had he been twenty years younger, this little dynamic package of female would likely have interested him as a woman to spend time with. But it was not twenty years ago. It was now, and there were deep, dark reasons why the handle Suicide had clung to him.

And there was a woman in his life back in America.

An extraordinary woman who also happened to be his CIA control officer; the one sustaining glimmer of hope and faith remaining in his existence of life and death and violence.

Her name was Sara.

CHAPTER FOUR

To Sara Durrell, a glass ceiling wasn't a limit. It was an obstacle to be smashed. Sara's way had been to pop off a few rounds into that glass ceiling—metaphorically speaking, of course—so she could kick her way right on through it.

In plain English, Sara was a former spy and covert ops field agent who rose through the CIA ranks to a top administrative position. At age thirty-four she was in shape and liked to think of herself as attractive enough. She'd fought her way up the rungs of the bureaucratic ladder in the epitome of a "good old boys' club", one of the few women to be promoted from field agent to liaison officer without enduring the usual "female" routes of serving as desk analyst or computer button pusher. Her promotions were hard earned from having risked life and limb in covert operations around the world.

Sara had survived those dangerous missions in diverse hostile environments because from the start she'd cultivated the habit of always remaining constantly aware of her surroundings. It wasn't a skill that diminished with the passage of time. And it was serving her well at the present moment.

Before her, a gathering of thousands sat silently enthralled by a forceful speech being delivered by the dynamic woman who paced alone across the vast stage as she spoke. The capacity crowd was hanging on the woman's every word, delivered in a husky voice so strong it was as if she needed no amplification to be heard from the stage thousands of feet away from where Sara stood, listening and observing at the rear of the enormous hall.

Thelma Justice wore a stylish but conservative black pants suit, a long body jacket shaped to complement the straight leg pants. She'd here come in simple makeup and a plain, conservative hairstyle, having learned long ago how to maximize and minimize her attractiveness as needed, a skill handed down by an uncle who had also served as an Agency field agent in his time. Her uncle had taught her the ability to be the person with a face no one noticed or remembered. The tricks were passed down to an attentive niece who also knew the skills of contouring brushes and eye shadow.

For Sara, this evening was a one-person reconnaissance and intel gathering operation. The CIA was not supposed to be operating on American soil. As such, she had come here tonight as a private citizen without a firearm . . . although she was armed with a knife disguised as a comb inside the discrete right pocket of her slacks.

"For too long," the woman on the stage was saying, "toxic masculinity has held a stranglehold upon the growth and potential of humanity!"

Thelma Justice was in her mid-40s, well preserved, well dressed and stylish in presentation and delivery; an energetic, personable, almost folksy manner just beneath the surface of vitriolic rhetoric. This blend of homespun mannerisms, watered down Eastern philosophy and the growing cult of her personality had engaged millions over the past decade. This "Justice Rally" was a yearly event that had grown bigger every year.

The attendance capacity of the convention hall was being sorely tested. Sellout crowds were nothing new for Ms. Justice, as she was commonly referred to. The Order of Harmony was comprised mostly of women. The quasi-religious group numbered its membership in the millions worldwide.

From humble beginnings, Ms. Justice—Sara was somewhat surprised to learn that was actually the woman's real name—had exploded onto the international scene to become the first true crossover media megastar of the 21st Century, embodying a feminist appeal that cut across racial, cultural and economic lines. Ms. Justice became one of the most influential women on the planet; not only a feminist icon but a titan of modern global industry. She was the third richest woman on Earth.

Workshops established around the world formed the basis of a movement more powerful than Scientology. Her obsession with privacy eclipsed the eccentricities of Howard Hughes and L. Ron Hubbard just as her global influence outdistanced theirs. Practically nothing was known about the woman's private life, most of which was spent behind the impregnable walls of her chalet/fortress high in the Italian Alps where an all-woman paramilitary force maintained security.

Sellout crowds were nothing new for the media mega star. Her daily network afternoon television show had been appointment television for millions of Americans either at home or in waiting rooms across the nation before she bowed out, with considerable fanfare, to start up her own network. On her very word, a novel would skyrocket to the top of the New York Times bestseller list or a small business product would become the hottest thing on the market. People she knew and respected found themselves hosting their very own talk shows and podcasts with her backing.

Sara found her mind wandering as Thelma Justice continued to enthrall her audience with what was, at its core, a decent motivational speech. She tried to stay focused but her restless spirit of her nature exerted itself and eventually she found her way out of the crowded hall to take in the comparatively fresh evening air outside. Ms. Justice had enough pull these days to rent the convention center's entire three acres for this Order of World Harmony conference.

Sara strolled almost idly along the rows of booths, most of which were getting a heavy play from conference attendees. Sara wandered without pausing to browse at any of the booths.

There were booths offering educational videos and literature on the struggle for equal rights in an age of patriarchy. Neighboring booths offered a myriad of products designed to encourage and instruct women in severing their reliance on the whims of toxic masculinity. Sara was sympathetic to this message of feminist empowerment and found herself genuinely and favorably impressed. Thelma Justice was contributing her wealth and prestige toward manifesting true equal rights in the world.

The more Sara walked, the more restless she became. She was here tonight on nothing more than a hunch; a sense that tonight was the confluence of something yet without parameters or real substance beyond pestering her subconscious. Or was she just mentally manufacturing thoughts and actions to distract her from concerns that would not let her go?

She had long ago accepted that she was an empath. Gift or curse, it wasn't something she summoned. It was something that was a part of her since the day she was born; empathy for that handful of people who mattered most to her. She worried about the people she cared most about. Her professional relationships were just that. Professional. The field agents and assets around the world that she directed from behind her desk at Langley all knew the risks they were taking when they signed on, same as herself. They were professionals doing a job, and so was she.

With one exception.

She'd known Jack Cody since before their professional association, before she'd become his immediate superior as control officer. She knew Jack Cody for damn sure. This was no ordinary man. For one thing, while he was more of a 100% "man's man" than any guy she knew, Cody had never once balked at having to take orders from a woman. Sara had been the best friend of Cody's lovely wife, Carol.

Jack's deceased wife.

Carol had worked at a mid-level administrative position at CIA Headquarters in Langley, Virginia which was where and how their three paths first converged. Cody and Carol fell in love, got married and had three kids. Sara was godmother to their children. Sara had been the last person Carol Cody spoke to before she died. An innocuous, kind of silly phone conversation between two old friends. Brief because Carol said she was on her way out the door, taking the kids to school.

Carol had gotten behind the wheel of the family car

and turned the key in the ignition, triggering a fiery explosion that killed her and the children in one shattering eruption of unthinkable violence and loss. The high explosive had been wired to the starter.

Cody went rogue after that. He settled the score with the terrorist scum who thought the bomb would kill him. It was months before he was returned to duty and, because Cody was the best they had and because approval of his reinstatement came straight down from the president, Cody was back on the job with only one catch. He would only accept missions classified as likely suicide missions. Sara could see it had something to do with survivor guilt, with a tormented soul wanting to rejoin his wife and children in the hereafter. He became Suicide Cody.

And she was the one sent him on those missions.

In fact, on a few of his recent missions she had gone into the field with him. This was gravely frowned upon by her superiors who would have blown a gasket had they known she and Cody were drawn together physically during one of those missions. Physically, as in lovers. It was one of those things and after it happened between them, their feelings for each other naturally deepened but always with the underlying tacit agreement between them: they were professionals and each had dedicated their life to their work.

All well and good. But on a mission like the one to take down General Greb Vetrov, she worried about the man she loved no matter how hard she tried to suppress it. She wondered how Cody was doing. He'd gone radio silent, as he usually did, but not before stating that he'd narrowed down Greb Vetrov's storage station for the weapons and the means by which he intended to transport them.

"Going alone is too much, even for you," she'd said in their last communication across the secure line.

"I have help," Cody had assured her. "Local asset. Kid named Tanya Lubyanka. She's one helluva wheelman."

Sara had looked her up immediately after they disconnected. Tanya Lubyanka was the university educated, strong-willed daughter of a regional lumber baron who was totally unaware of his daughter's activities. The girl had proven her worth on previous ops working with other agents, and was rated as an impeccable asset. Much as Sara would have preferred providing Cody with a contingent of Navy SEAL commandos to back his play, she understood the name of the game and how Cody played it.

She understood Cody, and that's where the concern came from. She worried about her guy. The romantic affection that flowed between her and Cody was good for her, heck yes. Sara told herself, *Give it a name, brave girl.* She was in love with Jack Cody and she was gratified to see that what flowed between them, whatever you called it, was helping to heal the man's damaged, torn-apart soul. She saw that during the off duty times they spent together when Cody was between ops. He was gradually showing signs of remembering how to relax and give again.

But he still only took on those damn suicide missions . . .

When she handed him those assignments, was she in reality enabling a man who deep down wanted to commit suicide?

Suddenly Sara stopped thinking about her man. Her sixth sense quivered.

She was being watched.

CHAPTER FIVE

SHE PAUSED at an author's booth, pretending to idly pick up a paperback.

A pair of women wearing khaki uniforms appeared in her peripheral vision. They seemed to be eyeing her with an intense scrutiny, their eyes hidden behind dark glasses. They were armed with Glock pistols in leather holsters along with collapsible batons, Tasers and nylon cable tie restraints.

Sara had first observed similarly attired women stationed as a line of security standing before the stage in the convention hall where Ms. Justice was delivering her address, and they were also posted here and there about the conference grounds.

Thelma Justice was renowned for having developed one of the world's first all-female security services. The Furies of Harmony were part of The Order of World Harmony. The pair Sara had noticed would be equipped with hands-free radio headsets, transparent polymer coils threaded from powerful, efficient radios to ear buds that served as both concealed speaker and contact microphone. One breath of warning, and the Furies' tac net would be alive and aware.

Sara had taken a look at their comm setup before coming here tonight. Easy enough to do as its layout had to be filed with and approved by the Federal Communications Commission. While she couldn't listen in on the encrypted network, just assessing its technology and the main radio command center was enough to determine that security here was anything but a second or third-rate operation. Topflight coordination and security measures were in place. Nothing short of an EMP pulse could interrupt the stream of communications among the Furies.

One wrong move of any kind and it wouldn't be a single security guard one had to worry about but an armed and coordinated team that would converge to outflank you and tighten the noose around your neck at the first sign of trouble. Figuratively speaking, one hoped.

The two Furies moved on. They'd noted Sara like they were checking out everyone passing by. Sara had done her best to not stand out visually or in any other way. Those Furies had lost interest in her but Sara kept an eye on them. They were on full alert, and the last thing she needed was to seriously attract their attention.

While she had no official sanction, her objective this evening was to connect with a specific person. She was following through on a vague but intriguing thread of intel, forwarded by her assets in the Mideast, concerning a 27-year-old Arab princess.

Princess Sheikha Aisha bint al-Ahmad was one of thirty children of a minor but prosperous member of the ruling family of one of the smaller city-states that comprised the United Arab Emirates. The princess was rather famous, trending virally with a rabid following numbering in the millions via Twitter, Instagram and other platforms where she was rumored to have associated herself with Thelma Justice.

Sara had utilized her CIA resources to track the princess here tonight. It was often the vague, whispered threads of intel that led to something substantial.

Aisha was a legitimate princess who had lived her life behind high walls. Despite the luxury of 40 rooms spread over four wings with hundreds of servants, the young woman's life had been one of enforced, confined leisure against which she'd always rebelled, drawing attention and raising controversy even in her younger days.

The Arab world was still very much a chauvinist culture. The 21st Century had little influence or effect on the bastion of masculinity that Thelma Justice despised with such passion in her feminist crusade. Teenaged Aisha endeavored to leave her country and infiltrate into Oman where she'd have gotten more leeway to support efforts for women's rights in the Middle East. A commando team sent by her father snatched Aisha up almost immediately and the girl found herself imprisoned in a minimum security camp designed to re-educate women who had lost their way.

Now, nearly ten years later, Princess Aisha had recently gone missing again, this time from her security detail on a trip to England. Her oldest brother, Achmed, has been dispatched by their father to retrieve the princess and return her by any and all means. The young woman's disappearance had lit up the whisper-stream of RUMINT and HUMINT—rumors and human intelligence–focused in the UAE. Sara's assets reported that it was whispered the Princess had come into possession of an artifact which possessed the potential to alter the modern world.

Sara admired Aisha's ability to ditch her bodyguards. A decade was a long time to wait for the perfect time and for professionals to lower their guard. The Princess had ghosted the team after only a few days in England. Somewhere out in the world, her brother Prince Achmed and his men were tracking every possible lead to locate the princess and bring her home whether she wanted to return or not. Whether the urgency was to silence a royal voice from speaking out against institutional sexism, or the recovery of her mysterious artifact, Sara didn't know. In any circumstance, Aisha's desire to bring modern human rights to the royal houses of the Arab world was just one tantalizing crumb on her trail that fueled Sara's interest.

Every professional instinct in Sara told her that Aisha would be here tonight, one of the thousands of attendees, somewhere amid this sprawling acreage. It was better than spending her off duty time alone with nothing else to do but worry about Jack Cody.

Back in the day when Thelma Justice she was still a daily magnet for a global audience attention with her satellite TV talk show, Princess Aisha had been the subject of several investigative episodes of her show. Ms. Justice championed a campaign to evoke international law in demanding the girl's release. This, the princess had said in a recent podcast from an undisclosed location, had contributed greatly in her joining the Order of World Harmony.

The princess would hardly be out in the open, not if she'd made contact with Ms. Justice. The Princess Aisha would be too valuable a resource for the Justice organization to leave her unattended. And so Sara was here with eyes and instincts peeled. There were areas of high security throughout the place as well as sentries whose vigilance was unyielding. Sara reminded herself that she must balance curiosity and inquisitive instincts with stealth. She had come here tonight to hopefully seek out and speak with Aisha one on one to determine what was so special about her artifact, and eke out any extra information about the girl's family in Dubai that she was so keen to disappear from.

Then, without warning, responding to something heard across their tac net, the two nearby Furies of Harmony burst into action.

CHAPTER SIX

IN THEIR LUXURIOUS PENTHOUSE SUITE, Windy Duke sent the email which Thelma Justice had just completed dictating.

The reasons for these annual events were many, not least among them the recruitment of VIP converts to the Order of World Harmony. The recipient of this "friendly, personal note" from Ms. Justice was little more than form, really, mandated by the million-dollar contribution to the Order signed over that afternoon from this recent convert.

Seated on a plush couch across from Wendy, Thelma observed Windy execute a quick scroll before closing her tablet.

Thelma asked, "Anything from 12-B?"

"Nothing yet."

"They were instructed to inform me the moment the princess arrives. I don't wish to be perceived as waiting for her but I should put in my appearance directly after she arrives."

"You know how it is with these affairs," said Windy.

"There's been some minor delay, nothing serious. Everything will go as planned."

Thelma fired up a cigarette, something she'd never been seen doing in public. She leaned her well-coiffed head back against the plush couch cushion.

"You're a blessing, Windy," she said with a sigh, "the way you always keep the show on track. You're a true friend. A true blessing."

"Just doing my job, ma'am," said Windy with a smile in the gruff, mock tone of a hired hand.

That's exactly what she was in her capacity as Thelma Justice's personal assistant and chief of staff. Windy basked in the complement. At an attractive and in-shape 36, she was dedicated to her present position. This was not a job, nor her duty. Spending her life in the service of Thelma Justice and the great woman's cause was Windy's blessing, much as the Order of World Harmony was divinity's blessing upon the world.

Windy had made certain that Thelma's every need was installed in their suite. This temporary headquarters of the far-flung Order was an internet hotspot capable satellite phone, tablets and a personal laptop all fit within one bag. Travel was generally in one of the Order's fleet of private jets but Thelma also dressed during travel in a far more subdued manner than usual, enabling her to travel in public without notice. Glasses and good wigs further kept her out of the limelight and stifled the efforts of paparazzi from unwanted intrusion into her affairs.

For anyone else it would have been impossible to believe that the woman who had just finished dictating her a letter, all cool business professionalism, was in fact the same dynamic public speaker fresh from having incited a crowded hall of devotees just a short time ago.

But Windy had been the "right hand woman" to this incredible, complex visionary long enough to appreciate the nuance of Ms. Justice's every mood and pattern of behavior. She worshipped the woman.

Thelma said, "I'll take that shot now."

Windy promptly went about fixing the drink.

She sensed an undercurrent of anticipation in her employer. It was not Windy's way to ask questions. She knew quite a bit about the behind the scenes doings of the Order of World Harmony, yet in many matters Thelma was a guarded, secretive person underneath her open smile and the strong, wise image she presented in public.

Wasn't it curious that a millionairess high roller should receive a template email in acknowledgment of her mega donation while a young woman from Dubai is being treated like, well, royalty? Windy knew of the Princess Aisha, of course, from the checkout stand tabloids when Windy did their shopping. Curiosity had been pestering her all day.

She handed the shot of vodka to Ms. Justice.

"Should I call to see what's holding her up?"

Thelma threw back the shot and returned the glass to Windy.

"Not at all, dear. Not proper to appear overly anxious, you know."

Windy's cell pinged. She glanced at the text message.

She said, "The princess has arrived at the reception in Meeting Room 12-B."

"Very good," said Thelma, "but we shall take our time. I could use another snort."

"Coming right up," said Windy.

"I haven't told you about this artifact she's bringing with her, have I, dear?"

Windy served her the shot.

"I've only seen it referred to when archiving your correspondence with her. It must be terribly important."

"Indeed it is. It will alter the future of the world." Thelma threw back the shot. "Do you remember the Knights Templar?"

"A force at the time of the Crusades, weren't they? The source of many myths and legends about missing treasure."

Thelma continued with a nod.

"All of the Templars in France were arrested for heresy by King Philip IV in 1307. Pope Clement dissolved the order in 1312. Did you ever wonder what heresy could have united a King and a Pope in destroying a religious order?"

"If I recall," said Wendy, "wasn't it something about a line of kings that could be traced directly back to a coupling between Jesus, the Son of God, and his lover, Mary Magdalene?"

"That is one possibility," said Thelma. "Here's another. Removing kings would be a means by which one could shake the foundations of the entire religious world. The Templars' worship at the altar of Baphomet is thought to have been code for something else. Baphomet is a gender-fluid creation, possessing both male and female anatomy which to the Catholic Church under Clement was an abomination. But it may well have been code for a belief system in which both men and women were recognized as possessing equal power under God. The Church also accused the knights of homosexuality which many scholars consider the means by which female knights of the Temple were eliminated. The Knights Templar had been raided and stripped of their supposed wealth, even though the entire order had always been depicted as being a group pledged to poverty. Two knights would share one horse. Two women could ride the same horse and since they wore armor, laymen wouldn't know the difference."

Windy's eyes widened.

"They sound like our Furies. So the Templars weren't all men?"

"Exactly." Thelma smiled, warming to her subject. "The Knights Templar, you see, was a slap in the face of the then-current toxic, masculine power of the Church. Even the most 'forward thinking' of Protestants believe in women being subservient when, quite the contrary, during the Crusades those women Templars were warriors for God, the voices of God on Earth."

"That's remarkable."

Thelma extinguished her cigarette. She rose from the couch with the leisure grace of a stirring lioness.

She said, "Remarkable enough to splinter the Vatican. And if it's true that the Templars did hide an enormous treasure, so much the better for our efforts."

"I think I'm beginning to understand."

"You do understand, darling. It will take money to tear down the system of enslavement that is global capitalism. What if the richest one percent in this world suddenly were faced with the poor of the world in possession of enough gold to shatter poverty? The rich, as we know, require the workers of the world to be despondent, dependent, so as to sustain and maintain their corrupt power of evil. They require a workforce willing to enslave themselves to corporations for the barest of sustenance and shelter. Our destiny is to destroy patriarchy to rebuild a world of true gender equality and harmony. The story of the Knights Templar being a matriarchal society will do much toward that end and will finance our cause once my resources are brought to bear in locating that Templar fortune. The truth of history is what Princess Aisha is said to have in her possession; what she intends to contribute to our cause."

"It sounds like a remarkable gift."

Windy always considered herself blessed to hear this great woman express her thoughts like this, one on one.

"It is most assuredly," agreed Thelma with a nod. "The Catholic Church is known to be in possession of thousands of years of stolen treasures from colonial conquest, including entire libraries of ancient knowledge. The medical secrets hidden under the guise of preventing witchcraft alone would be enough to wipe clean the morass which is the modern medical industry. Can you imagine a world where cancer has a cure that's been buried before we even had a name for the series of diseases? A world where chemotherapy and radiotherapy are no longer needed and cancer's victims don't spend billions a year and suffer from chemical and radiation poisoning?"

Thelma reached for her purse, checking herself in the foyer wall mirror and satisfied with what she saw.

"Too long has the face of society and progress been a pale, wrinkled mask of insecure masculinity. With the materials that Aisha's artifact will provide, I shall cast a new reality wherein the white male must face his true status as a minority. By the blades of the warrior women of the Temple, by their blessed teachings excised from the Bible by an egotistical British king who wanted to erase women and any hint of non-Europeans from the Holy Book, by all of this combined, I—*we*—shall take this world and guide it into an age of true enlightened equality.

"Think of all the societies shunned by the precursor

of the male of our species. The Amazons. The Furies. The Shield Maidens of the Vikings. The thousands of women of the Tai Ping Tian Guo movement in China. The Japanese Onna-musha who were the equals of the samurai. And now, the Templars. Not male homosexual devil worshippers but *women* who rejected the masculine indoctrination of a gender-blind Pope. We shall raise ourselves, our planet, on the shoulders of the witches fanatics failed to burn, and all of the female warriors throughout history who refused to resign themselves to being barefoot and pregnant. Straight white men have butchered holy messages to maintain their supremacy. They are the enemy. Those truly good of heart and those willing to learn, male and female, will always have a sacred place in any world. But we are the ones who have already manifested an army of strong women across the globe; the guardians of this coming enlightened age."

Windy said, "An ancient artifact that substantiates this history will inspire millions."

Thelma started toward the door, fully expecting Windy to step past and open the door for her. She said, "My destiny is nothing less than to command extremes of the universe. I only hope this reception for the princess doesn't drag on." Her words took on a throaty, personal tone. "I have one more scheduled guest coming tonight that I haven't told you about. The one who keeps our Furies in the newest and finest of weaponry and equipment . . . and who keeps your Ms. Justice satisfied between the sheets," she added with a course chuckle.

Windy made no comment. The great lady was certainly entitled to a personal life. Windy's phone pinged when she was halfway to the door. She frowned at the caller ID and answered. She frowned as she listened and the frown deepened when she ended the brief call.

"What is it?" Thelma asked, reading her expression.

"It's the reception in 12-B," Windy said as if out of breath. "Something terrible has happened!"

CHAPTER SEVEN

THE TWO FURIES of Harmony blew past Sara in a fast walk. A comment passed between them reached Sara's ears. Something about Meeting Room 12-B.

Sara referred to her mental map of the facility and locked onto their destination, one of the restricted areas that had aroused her interest: not a large conference room, it would have perfectly served as a "green room" to accommodate a special guest like Princess Aisha. She followed the two Furies, maintaining her distance from them.

More Furies of Justice came jogging into the building housing Meeting Room 12-B, their hands on the grips of their holstered pistols. Sara resisted the urge to break into a jog as she entered the building after them, keeping her hand away from the comb knife hidden in her pocket.

Things were in motion! No less than a dozen security personnel had shown up thus far. Even as she stalked along after the Furies, Sara spotted something out of the corner of her eye. Situational awareness hadn't let her down.

A lovely young Arab woman, with flowing black hair and darkly luminous skin, came toward her, hurrying away in the opposite direction as the converging Furies. She wore a backpack, jeans and a surplus army jacket that did much to disguise her lithe figure. With the benefit of having studied dozens of photographs of the princess, Sara ID'ed her from the jawline, the shape of her nose and the outline of eyes through dark sunglasses that hid the expression in those eyes.

To a trained eye there was no doubting her intention. The princess was determined to distance herself from the excitement behind her, striding briskly with that grace of one who'd come of age as a professional equestrian athlete. Expensive riding boots confirmed that impression.

Sara broke off from tailing the Furies, altering her course to intercept the princess.

It was during a horseback ride on her father's estate outside London that Aisha had gone missing this time around. One moment, the security detail assigned to her had her in their sights. The next, she'd galloped off into the heavily forested woodland. Even utilizing a helicopter, a drone and ATVs, the royal guard lost her. The horse was found eating grass and drinking from a water fountain in a garden in a small town miles from the Ahmad estate. The princess was nowhere to be found.

The young woman approaching her was walking with shoulders hunched, tugging her hair into a ball that went under the hood of her sweatshirt. Had she drawn up the hood sooner, Sara might not have identified her. It was a safe bet that Aisha had just now exited Meeting

Room 12-B and in extreme haste. She was still adjusting her clothing to further disguise her appearance.

Sara spoke up.

"Excuse me, miss." The princess kept on walking as if she hadn't heard, her face downcast, shadowing her features beneath the hood. Sara said, "Aisha?"

The princess stopped at that, her shoulders tensed. She half turned to Sara. There was the faintest coppery scent of fresh blood about her. Speckles of red were drying on her shirt front.

"Who are you?"

The response was quiet, fearful. Sara extended an arm and looped their elbows together, steering them along away from the meeting room area.

"Princess, who are you running from? I can help."

Aisha regarded her intently as they walked.

"Who are you?" she asked again. "How much do you know?"

She disengaged her arm from Sara's. Sara paced with her, glancing behind them. The Furies gathered around the meeting room entrance were occupied, far from earshot.

She said, "Tell me first what happened in that meeting room? Is your brother, Achmed, here tonight? Is he the one you're running from?"

"He couldn't find me here," Aisha said, but she sounded doubtful as if trying to convince herself. "Achmed's men wouldn't dare try anything in such a public place. Father would never allow that."

She was still taking her measure of this woman who'd accosted her; tentative and uncertain, but wanting to hear more.

"I came here looking for you," said Sara. "I found you."

"But why?"

"Don't be alarmed, Aisha. I'm with the US government." Sara told the girl her name. "Your disappearing act has raised a lot of flags not only with your father but also here in America."

She was pitching the approach cool and conversational. It seemed the best way, under these spontaneous circumstances, to counter the raw, quivering emotion readily apparent this close up. The smell of violence about Princess Aisha and the fresh freckles of blood, now again concealed, had been enough. Aisha was on that traumatic brink of losing it that can befall a civilian after exposure to an act of extreme violence.

Aisha spoke as if in a trance.

"Two of the Furies assigned to protect me . . ." Her words faltered. ". . . they're dead!" Trauma dripped from her every word. "I've never seen someone killed before. It's . . . it's nothing like the movies . . ."

"Can you describe the assailants?"

"They were dressed like . . . like normal people. Goggles. A Fury guard . . . pushed me out through an emergency exit." Tears trickled from under Aisha's sunglasses, crystals shining on her caramel cheeks. "She shielded me. I felt her fall against me. I ran and when I had gotten away, I started walking before anyone could respond."

Aisha's riding boots clacked with the same sharp pace as Sara's shoes on the tile floor.

"Not a bad strategy," said Sara. "Let's keep moving."

"You said you could help me."

"I can but I have to know more. I didn't hear any gunfire. Were they using silencers?"

The hoodie shook once in the negative.

"Not bullets. Arrows. They attacked us with *arrows!*"

Aisha's English was impeccable but under stress like this, sometimes translations didn't break across the mental barriers erected by trauma.

"Crossbows?" Sara asked.

"Yes, crossbows! Small, like toys, concealed under their jackets. But powerful, very powerful. The ones who attacked us . . . they were after me. The Furies who were assigned to accompany me . . . they were all killed with the crossbows, all of them. It . . . it was *horrible!*"

The princess clutched her fatigue jacket lapels together, concealing the bloodstains, when several more Furies of Harmony hurried past.

Intent on reaching the meeting room, none of these paused to cast a glance at the pair of seemingly innocent, unaware and unassuming ladies. Sara thought no less of the top-flight security. In combat it's called the fog of war. First responders to horror brought training into the fog of chaos.

Sara did overhear one of the Furies speaking to another as they rushed past.

"...no sign of intruders . . ."

After these Furies were gone, Sara said to Aisha, "If they're still on the grounds, they've already ditched their crossbows. They got as close to you as they did because, like me, they're not packing heat so they draw attention. With any luck, they're long gone." Sara's intuition pushed another thought to the surface. "How did you get here tonight, Princess?"

"The Order. They have been helping me since I broke free in the UK. Ms. Justice is a great woman, doing great things. I have something for her that will do much to help the cause."

Sara thought, *Spoken like a true cultist.* By this time

they were leaving the building, stepping outside into the well-lighted rows of dealers' booths.

Sara said, doing her best to sound nonchalant, "The gift you brought her. You're referring to the artifact?"

"Oh no," said Aisha.

At first it seemed like her response.

But it was more a startled gasp of alarm. Aisha drew up sharply, staring straight ahead at a heavily muscled young man who stood squarely in their path as if waiting for them.

Attired in unassuming casual clothes, the only indication that he was more than a bystander was that, behind his mirrored aviator shades, his attention was focused like a laser solely on them. His hands were empty, and he did not display an aggressive stance. His feet were perpendicular to each other in a T-stance, a martial arts stance that made him extremely difficult to be toppled, providing superior mobility.

Aisha lifted a trembling finger and pointed at the man.

"He's one of them! He killed the one who was shielding me!"

He came at them fast, displaying no weapon other than his calloused hands and his feet. The setup was easy enough to read. The attempt in the meeting room went sour so here was their backup and he likely wasn't alone. Sara read stone cold death in his eyes.

She dropped to the side with a frightened little yelp, positioning herself behind Sara who drew the comb-knife from its pocket.

The guy lifted a blocking arm in response to the quick draw, twisting aside when her blade slashed through the sleeve of his jacket. A stream of his blood splashed the air. He drew back with a start of surprise, wincing in pain.

Sara was already drawing Aisha along with her, guiding the princess in a hurried withdrawal. Around them, onlookers who'd witnessed the sudden confrontation were reacting, their cries of shock and surprise filling the air. Sara's goal was to lose their assailant in the complex of booths. She kept the lethal steel knife low against her leg so as to not draw further attention as they scrambled to get away.

Another man loomed in front of them. A tall form that appeared like a spire amid a stormy ocean of humanity. A big fist at the end of a long arm swung at Sara. The blow was too swift to avoid in all of the confusion. His punch caught her on the jaw and set Sara's world a-spinning. Blood roared in her ears.

She slashed up with the knife in counterattack. The blade snagged on this man's clothing. Then a knee was kicked out from under her, the leg blazing with pain, instantly numb. A follow-through karate chop lashed at her biceps, the impact numbing her hand, causing the comb knife to drop from nerveless fingers. Sara struggled to stay standing, blocking a punch with her good hand.

The dude's follow-through punch collided with the side of her skull.

Sara dropped. The pavement smacked her. She summoned the strength she needed to regain an unsteady footing. She tasted blood in her mouth. She felt woozy as hell, people with blurred faces in a dizzy motif were dancing across her vision.

The assailants had both run off, losing themselves amid the crowd around the booths.

Aisha was nowhere to be seen.

This being the 21st century in urban America, no one

came forward to offer assistance, everyone assuming this was some sort of domestic drama playing itself out in public. No one wanted to get involved.

That suited Sara just fine. She limped away, barely holding it together. The world kept tilt-a-whirling like she was seeing the northern lights from an out of control merry-go-round. She had to center her total concentration to simply keep walking away from there. One step at a time. One step after another. She kept pushing herself. She kept walking.

She could barely see straight. Every light had its own halo. She didn't know where she was, for how long she walked, only that eventually she stepped into the deep shadows of an alley, oddly detached from the noise and sights whirling about her. She sat heavily on the ground, drawing her phone from a jacket pocket.

Dimly she became aware of people gathering about her, some of them starting to ask if she was okay. She started to dial her phone. She tasted blood on her lips.

Then she slumped into unconsciousness.

CHAPTER EIGHT

THE UNMARKED AGENCY car was waiting for Cody
when his flight touched down. A four-door Cad with
tinted windows, its license plate bore the official government stamp. Sara usually sent a ride along as a convenience upon his return to Washington following a
mission. The rear passenger door yawned, opened by
whoever sat inside.

So who was here to meet him besides the chauffeur?

Not Sara, who never personally came to the airport
to greet him. Not professional, she said. And as in most
things, she was right.

He walked around the rear of the vehicle. The
pleasant warm spring sunshine of D.C. was a welcome
change from the bone-deep chill of the Urals and the
recycled air of the long series of connecting diplomatic
flights that brought him home. The trunk clicked open,
activated from inside the car by the chauffeur. Cody
stowed his suitcase in the Cadillac's trunk.

The Beretta traveled in a secret compartment of the
suitcase. If trouble was waiting for him in the car, what

the hell. He'd just blown a train off the tracks and to kingdom come halfway across around the world. Trouble in the enclosed confines of an automobile, in daylight in a public parking lot, was nothing to worry about.

He slid into the rear seat. AC cool and shiny dark leather embraced him.

A slim, bespectacled, sandy haired guy sat stiffly at the far end of the bench seat. Not much past thirty. Cody recognized him but only vaguely. Jared P-something or other. A Company pencil pusher on his way up the ladder at Langley. He sported a buzz cut that made him look right out of boot camp.

"Parnell. Jared Parnell," he said in a voice as stiff as his posture, without extending his hand. "We need to talk, you and me."

Charming, thought Cody.

He said, "I'm listening. But I'll be honest. Right now my mind's on getting a long hot shower and a good American cheeseburger. Why are you here, Parnell, and why can't it wait?"

"A list of reasons," said Parnell. He placed an electronic cigarette to his lips and inhaled. The water vapor steamed from his nostrils as if he were an idling dragon, filling the car's interior with its scent of sickly sweet false tobacco. "You let Vetrov slip through your fingers."

"But I did derail his shipment of nukes. The hunt for the general is still on. New intel will push that along soon enough. What else?"

"There's your girlfriend, Sara Durrell." He snickered at the word girlfriend. "She screwed up royally before she was hospitalized. I suspect you're a part of whatever hustle she was up to. We're keeping a close eye on that woman."

Cody's gut muscles began to tense. He countered this

with a yoga-trained breath, dispelling the anger that bubbled within him, breathing out measuring his words.

"What happened? Where are you keeping this eye on her?"

"Your pretty little chick broke protocol. Stuck her nose into activities she had no business investigating. She utilized unauthorized agency procedure and personnel to locate and track a private citizen on US soil. She's been summarily relieved of duty. I'm serving as her temporary replacement. In other words, Cody, I'm your control officer. As a result of her activities, Ms. Durrell was assaulted and beaten just this side of death by a person or persons unknown."

"I said, where is she?"

Parnell sucked another hit off his e-cigarette, exhaling scented steam through a malicious smirk.

"That information is need-to-know. You've got your own troubles, old-timer. Improper fraternization with a coworker. A guy with your mileage ought to know better. Screw around with your fellow agents, you could end up going to their funerals. I've undertaken the task of cleaning up this unit, Cody. You and Durrell are both up for serious reprimand."

"That's big talk, junior."

"Yeah, and I plan to deliver. I'm not intimidated by you. Suicide Cody. Only takes on death-wish missions where you're not expected to return. But you keep returning. You know, pal, around the watercooler a few of us have a pool going on when your ass *isn't* coming back. I thought for sure your trip to Russia would've done it."

"Vetrov's a loose end," said Cody. "I hate loose ends. This mission isn't over until the general goes down and stays down."

Parnell leaned in close, his hot breath cloying.

"If it was up to me, the Agency would've dropped a Maverick missile in that Russkie's lap."

"But you don't hold that kind of rank, do you, pencil pusher? Sounds like Sara took a hit and you're trying to turn that into another rung up the ladder for you. I don't like that, Parnell. I don't like you."

Parnell snorted. E-cigarette steam escaped his nostrils in a puff.

"You're a tough old dinosaur to ruffle, I'll give you that, Cody. Are you listening, grandpa? I'm on the way up and you're almost out the door. Your personal relationship with Durrell is highly inappropriate. You're too damn old school so I'm serving notice, okay? Your days in this agency are numbered. I'm lobbying to shut you down, Cody. We'll all be better off around here when 21st century efficiency takes over and you're dead and gone."

Cody thought, enough is enough. He leaned across the bench seat and fisted a firm hold of Parnell's necktie. With a forceful yank, he jerked the guy forward so they were nose to nose.

Parnell made a funny choking sound. His e-cigarette fell to the Cad's carpeted floor.

Cody said, slowly enunciating each word precisely, "Which hospital?"

"Cody . . . *let me go!* Are you crazy?"

Cody flicked his wrist, tightening the necktie into a strangling noose.

"Where?"

Parnell's hands lifted frantically, trying to loosen the necktie.

"Jeez, Cody, stop! You'll kill me . . ."

"Small loss," growled Cody. "Where is she, you little prick?"

"Walter Reed." The words came breathy through clenched teeth, Parnell's color becoming increasingly purple from loss of breath. "Bethesda . . . prison wing . . ."

Cody released his hold of the necktie with a shove that sent Parnell back to his side of the car.

"Why the prison wing?"

Parnell eyed him with the wary look of one who's angered a mountain lion.

"We've cut off access so she doesn't screw around with any more billionaires and Arab princesses. What . . . what are you going to do?"

Cody shifted his attention to the chauffeur. The man drove with his back straight, looking straight ahead as if deaf. But he wasn't deaf and Cody recognized him as one of Sara's regular drivers. Time to find out where his loyalties lay.

Cody said to the chauffeur, "Pull over. Mr. Parnell has decided to go for a walk."

Parnell was regaining his edge, straightening his tie and hair.

"Walk? I'm not walking anywhere."

The chauffeur was already gliding the Cadillac to a stop at the curb.

Cody said to Parnell, "You can let yourself out or I can assist you. You wouldn't like that."

Parnell took a moment to consider his response. Then he clicked open his door handle.

"You're going to regret this, Cody. You haven't seen the last of me. You and me are going to tango big time."

"Out," Cody repeated. When Parnell was gone, he said to the chauffeur, "Thanks."

The driver eased the Cad away from the curb, back into the traffic flow.

"Sir, I don't care for that gentleman. Ms. Durrell, she's fine woman. Where to, sir?"

Cody settled back against the plush black leather. His gut was in a tight knot.

"Bethesda Naval Hospital," he said, "and step on it."

CHAPTER NINE

AT ABOUT THE same time that Jack Cody was being airlifted out of Russia, Greb Vetrov, with confidence and a stony countenance, was approaching the magnificent Beletoz Tower in Moscow. One of his many cover business concerns rented offices there as well as storage lockers and safe deposit boxes on multiple levels of the Tower. His official ties here were tenuous; thin threads that only the most determined of investigators could ever hope to pin down and trace. And as yet, no one had.

Or had they?

He had a stalker. A tall, burly Russian male fitting a description not dissimilar to his own.

The Tower could well be under surveillance by not only the Russian authorities but maybe even by the Americans. His intended role camouflage, as he prepared to enter the magnificent building, relied on the sheer volume of office workers entering and leaving Beletoz Tower every minute of the workday. Four thousand permanent employees in the building, as well as those coming and going for appointments or shopping in the stores and restaurants that comprised the first four levels, accounted for an estimated additional three to five thousand people passing in and out of the building daily.

True, his was an unmistakable military bearing. But in Modern Russia, military veterans are everywhere.

With shoppers surging about him, Vetrov paused at a storefront, pretending to admire the display in its window while scanning for more trouble in the reflection of the glass. He detected a second tail on his paranoid radar among the flowing throng of people.

His shadows, their team included a stout woman, each had that sober, detached yet keenly observant appearance clearly stamping them as secret police. Could there be more than these two? *Come closer*, he found himself thinking. He continued to maneuver his way along the crowded sidewalk of the busy thoroughfare. Did these stalkers believe he was blithely walking into their trap?

He might well have been lured into an inescapable snare . . . that is, if he hadn't known the Beletoz Tower from the helipad on its roof down to the smallest wiring detail in the sub-basement. These agents were on *his* turf. He had a dozen escape routes already in place if he needed them, both around and throughout the towering structure. The Russian authorities thought that they had him? Ha! Should they post a cordon around Beletoz Tower, to Vetrov it would be nothing more than a sieve.

He was quicksilver.

A safe deposit box with money awaited him in that building. A forged passport. And his ticket on a commercial flight out of Russia under the alias of a persona created and crafted over the years well beneath the official radar. Before long he would be in Washington D.C. There he would relate the loss of those nuclear warheads while appeasing his woman with his sexual prowess. At this point in a lifelong pursuit of carnal pleasure, she was the only woman who had ever matched his ardor between the sheets . . .

All of this depended on his escape from Moscow and the dragnet. The Beletoz Tower seemed to touch the cloudy sky on this cool day. The building continued downward into the earth, providing access at one of its basement levels to the Moscow Metro train system. He would acquire what he needed at the station. And there he would make the government pay for this effort to stop him. He wanted his shadows to see where he was going.

He made his way not to the building's main entrance but further along the sidewalk to the busy stairway leading down to the Metro. He paused at the top of those stairs. One of the men was already making a beeline through the crowd, coming toward him.

Vetrov entered the stairway, at first merging with the human flow of travelers but then quickly sidestepping into an indented blind spot along the wall, knowing he'd find the door to the private service area. He elbowed through that door into a well-lit silence of vague echoes. The door swung closed on its hydraulic arm.

Vetrov drew back and waited.

In a moment, the door burst open again under a kick from the shadow, looking up and down the flights of stairs that led from this landing. A brief hesitation that left him easy prey. Vetrov came out of a dark corner to smash his forearm hard against the back of the man's neck. The fellow sailed forward from the force of the blow, his hands in a windmill of motion to maintain balance or grab a rail to prevent a tumble down the steep flight of metal stairs. Vetrov followed up with a savage punch to the kidney that robbed the strength from the man's legs.

The agent tumbled down the metal stairs, loud wet cracks resounding as his face crushed against the unyielding steps. When he reached the bottom of this flight, his head struck the cement landing and ended bent at an obscene angle. To make certain the bastard's neck was shattered, Vetrov slid down the railing and kicked down hard with both feet. Bones crunched, a reassuring pop and snap through the soles of his shoes. Vetrov followed up with one more savage stomp, and watched thick red globs of blood explode from the dead man's mouth.

He spent a quick moment frisking the man. He found a pistol and pocketed it but did not waste any more time on this landing. He descended the next flight of stairs.

The door above swung inward. A loud male curse echoed in the stairwell. The second of these men had found his partner. This one's footfalls rumbled down the stairs. Vetrov waited for him, concealed by a sharp dogleg in the steps leading. He waited, standing in the center of the landing, with his "borrowed" pistol aimed upward. As soon as the man's legs became visible, he squeezed the trigger, shooting the agent in the groin.

This fellow cried out, clutched himself and lost his balance on the stairs, tumbling over the handrail to join his deceased colleague.

Vetrov considered taking the time to make sure this one was finished too but no, a wounded agent would serve to slow down the others who were in pursuit. He continued on, concealing the pistol in his pocket. No need to cause panic or draw attention in the station. The stairwell had contained the barking of gunfire from nearby travelers focused solely on reaching their destination.

Rushing down the steps, exiting through another service door into the subway station without drawing a noticeable reaction from anyone, Vetrov was again swallowed at once by the crisscrossing streams of humanity earnestly hoofing to and from train platforms. The press of humanity was perfect camouflage. The arcades were busy, many pausing to browse at the newsstand shops and food stands lining the way, imbibing coffee and pastry to tide them over until a proper meal.

Vetrov blended in seamlessly, just one more face in the crowd, making his way toward a wall of secured lockers when he spotted another of the telltale agents. They were pulling out every stop possible, apparently, to the point of posting a man to exclusively keep an eye on the lockers. There would be still more agents close at hand.

Vetrov walked right past the agent. The man spotted him and fell in behind, at a distance, following him into the men's room. The instant Vetrov was inside, the foul closeness of the latrine enveloped him. He plucked a small dagger from a sheath worn at his calf. He swung around behind the privacy wall.

The door swung open with the entrance of the agent. Vetrov jumped him from behind, striking his elbow against the man's jaw with a stunning impact that threw the man to the floor. Vetrov immediately lunged in for the kill, the honed point of his steel blade sinking into the yielding flesh at the side of the man's neck. Scarlet claret fountained out from the arterial wound. The fellow clawed at his neck as if to stem the irrepressible flow but his hands were numb, his blood pressure diminishing by the second.

Vetrov took care to step well around the man's twitching remains. The spreading pool of blood glistened vividly in the high voltage overhead lighting. He exited the washroom. The bloody dagger dropped into the wastepaper receptacle on his way out, striding directly and intently toward his original destination. At the wall of lockers where travelers could temporarily store their belongings, he brought out the key his people had supplied him with. He opened the locker.

Inside the locker was a built-in deposit box. He switched keys, opened this second box and extracted the envelope he wanted from those it was nestled among. The envelope's thickness, the feel of the folded passbook under the manila, told him he had what he needed.

Tucking the envelope into an inside coat pocket, he rejoined the flow of humanity making its way toward the platforms. He took the long way around, this time skirting that service stairwell door when he happened to spot two agents emerging from there. He surveyed the escalators traveling down from street level, the unending parade of commuters providing an impenetrable wall to anyone who wanted to rush down in pursuit of him.

He brought up his electronic metro pass on his phone. Passing through the turnstile without hesitation, he allowed himself to remain highly observant and yet in a passive mode, allowing the massed movement of hurrying people to carry him forward toward the subway car that had just arrived.

Vetrov could not contain the fleeting inward hint of a smile that visited his stern visage.

He threw a look along his backtrack, up the escalator and there she was. The stout, brawny female plainclothes agent, seen even from this distance, stood out unmistakably in a crowd. She was trying to hurry, to shove people aside, but her proportions and aggression could not alter the basic laws of physics. People tried to get out of her way but the escalator's narrow dimensions additionally contributed to hampering her progress.

More bodies had swarmed between Vetrov and the agents from the stairwell. He was carried through the subway car's doors mere seconds before they closed with sudden finality. The subway car gave a jolt and they were on their way.

He was ahead of the opposition as usual!

THEN ONE OF the male agents made it to the doors only a fraction of a second after it had closed. The man beat a fist impotently against the window. Vetrov made eye contact with him and smirked. The man was now jogging along outside the accelerating train. He smirked right back. Then the service door at the far end of the car, connecting it to the next, slid open.

So that was it! One man distracts him while another leaps aboard another car and closes in through the clot of countless commuters. Considering their number and methodical organization, this unit could be nothing short of government sanctioned assassins!

Vetrov kept forcing his way through the subway car, shoving people aside. They reacted to the cold-blooded murder they saw in his eyes. The one advancing on him in the car encountered the same resistance as Vetrov thanks to the density of packed-in men and women riding the subway. Passengers kept trying to get out of the way but there were so many of them, the man was slowed enough not to gain on Vetrov. A few more moments and Vetrov reached the sliding door at this end of the car. He passed through, finding enough of an areaway between the cars to crouch in waiting.

The man came through. His eyes widened in surprise at finding his prey confronting him. He made a clawing grab for concealed hardware.

By that time Vetrov had already palmed and drawn a nasty little spade-shaped push-blade from its small, concealed scabbard on his belt. He brought his empty left hand up to seize the man's wrist that held the half-drawn gun. The push knife sank into the fellow's forearm like a warm knife sliding into butter, tearing cloth, muscle and blood vessels. The gun dropped from paralyzed fingers, connections from hand to brain severed with the deft blade work.

Vetrov closed in, jerking the man against him with force enough to nearly tear the assassin's arm from its socket. He skillfully plunged the fist knife into the exposed flesh of the man's throat. Feeling the slightest resistance of the tough, fibrous windpipe, Vetrov sank the blade in more forcefully. The undersized knife wouldn't cut through trachea but found its way out and to the side. Muscle parted, the blade slicing efficiently through the jugular vein and carotid artery. Vetrov withdrew the push knife again and rammed it into the man's belly.

The assassin's eyes glazed over as the blood flow to his brain was diverted out of his body. Coughing up a darkened stream of bile and stale plasma, he crumpled into an inert mass.

Vetrov smiled his pride at a job well done. These connecting doors were seldom if ever used by subway riders. The corpse would likely go undiscovered for a while at least. Vetrov stepped into the next car.

The train was taking him northwest toward Sheremetyevo Airport, but he intended from the start to switch trains at the next station and go south toward Moscow Domodedovo Airport, where his flight was booked and waiting. Within the hour he would be at Moscow Domodedovo, aboard the flight to the East Coast of the United States. Then he could relax and renew body and spirit with vodka cocktails to tide him over the ten hour journey.

CHAPTER TEN

SARA OPENED AN EYE.

Her other eye was taped shut to facilitate the healing of an orbital fracture. As she awoke, hospital sounds and scents became part of a once-removed awareness of human activity nearby, muddled as if smothered in cotton.

She was in her hospital room, hooked up to neck brace, bandages, IV tubes and whatnot. A hospital room with a difference. Her "room," normal and pleasant enough, was really a cell in the prison wing of Walter Reed Hospital. Armed guards patrolled the corridor outside her closed, locked door, the door made of steel with an electronic lock. She'd slipped into a medicated nap. She was thinking clearly only with effort.

Jack Cody occupied the single uncomfortable visitor chair under a high, barred window. His rock steady eyes were on her like a silent sentinel.

A surge of relief flowed through her and she automatically started to sit up, to get out of her hospital bed and embrace her man. An automatic reaction, yes. But she could not move! She'd forgotten about the padded restraints around her wrists and ankles and the belt across her midsection.

I'm a prisoner!

And it all came back in a rush. I'm locked up in a hospital room while armed killers are after a princess named Aisha. Why did they do this to *me*? Was it because she'd made contact with Aisha? Of course it was. But who was responsible? Middle Eastern royalty? Or a certain offended cult leader? Did it concern the historical artifact that was supposedly in Aisha's possession?

Or was it as Sara had originally suspected: a confluence of players and motives that ended up with Jared Parnell placing her in here while he applied personal ambition and design to the president's High Risk Task Force of which she and Cody were the core?

What a mess.

At least now she was fully awake from her "nap," cognizant of her situation and feeling that surge of uplift at the presence of this man regarding her from where he sat. Cody sat at attention, eyes steadily on her as she gradually regained consciousness.

Gauging the time by the sky beyond the window, Sara said, "Good afternoon."

"Is it?" Cody asked with one of his small smiles she knew so well.

Sara frowned.

"They're stingy with the pain medication so no, I wouldn't say it's a good afternoon at all. But it sure is nice to see you, big guy. Unless they're not so stingy and I'm so doped up to the gills and hallucinating that you're here. *Are* you really here, Cody?"

"I'm here, hon."

She yearned to fall into his arms for a bear hug

embrace and a few thousand kisses. Even in her present condition she would sure as hell be able to feel those strong arms wrapped around her. Arms that could handle anything. But no, she was manacled to the goddamn bed! The sense of oppression weighed down her spirit like a block of cement. She tried not to let it show.

"How long have you been sitting there?"

"Half hour, maybe. You were asleep when I got here. How're you feeling, Sara?"

"You must have laid on some fancy double talk to get yourself in to see me. My understanding is that I'm officially off limits."

"Not to me you ain't," Cody grinned. "I was hoping you'd stay out of trouble while I was gone."

She leaned across awkwardly to moisten her throat with a straw-sipped drink of water from the plastic water cup on the stand beside her. The slight movement this required brought on a wave of ache throughout her body. Resting her head on the pillow, Sara reached down and thumbed the control button, raising half the bed so she could look directly at Cody. She gave him a weak smile.

"How was Russia?"

"Too damn cold. The trains are pure murder."

Sara's gaze shifted to the blue sky pouring through the window. The glass was reinforced with black fibers of alloy wire that made the window virtually unbreakable to anything short of high explosives. Even from where she lay, she could see the two eavesdrop microphones embedded in the window frame. Undoubtedly more would have been installed around the room and in the john.

Cody said, "Your friend Jared met me at the airport."

"Figures. Sorry about that. Welcome home, Cody."

In her med-induced state, she could practically smell Parnell and his vape pen. She sneezed mightily at the imagined chemical stink. Felt like she was head butting a sledgehammer. She sighed. Even that hurt.

Cody was there for her with a tissue. She blew her nose, relieving the pressure of the sneeze. Cody appeared to naturally bring his lips close to her ear in the process. He softly murmured into her ear.

He spoke only a few words, low and quick, providing Sara a staging code for the rest of their conversation. And Sara's mind sprang into action.

Standard spycraft. A means by which they could share information. Of course the listeners would be prepared to recognize a cipher code in conversation. But that did not mean they would be able to break the code established between two individuals highly skilled at improvisation and deception.

To anyone else, the conversation that followed was two friends engaging in small talk about this or that. A well-versed, especially astute cinephile might have recognized banter from an old detective series of movies about a husband and wife couple who solved high society mysteries. Those movies had been a favorite of Sara's since she was a kid. She and Cody liked watching them together, especially enjoying the couple's fresh, bantering, sometimes suggestive rapport.

Sara would pause from time to time and let Cody have the floor regarding some prosaic detail while she blinked her eye in a Morse code to supply him with specific information. This conversation went on for twenty minutes. When it wound down, Sara had managed to inform Cody where she'd hidden her files in reference to Thelma Justice and Princess Aisha. She conveyed, amid what seemed to be boring chitchat, the warning that more than one group of rough customers were looking for Aisha. And she briefed Cody on the Furies of Harmony, concluding the info dump with an oblique reference to all of the additional complications posed by the girl's brother and his team.

Sara felt hamstrung. Sure, their code was impenetrable but she only had this one chance, camouflaged in movie quotes and mentions of the food and the staff here and what a complete asshole Jared Parnell was. All right, talking trash about Parnell wasn't such a bad thing. Felt good to get it out of her system. But the fact remained, here she was under heavy guard in this box of reinforced glass and electronic ears.

A series of clicks came from the hatch lock on the room's door. The door swung inward on its heavy-duty hinges and remained open.

Jared Parnell walked in.

Cody rose to his feet.

Sara sensed immediately the electric tension and dislike that coursed between these two. She had no idea what could've transpired at the airport today between them, but it hadn't been good. That was easy to see in Parnell's body language: balled fists, narrowed eyes, looking right off the bat like he wanted to take a swing at Cody.

The two of them made and held eye contact. There in the close-in confines of her room/cell, Parnell kept his distance from Jack Cody.

Parnell said, with an edge in his voice, "Visiting hours are over, big man."

Cody said, "I'll leave when I want to leave."

"Yeah, well you may not be leaving at all, bigshot. Not after that stunt you just pulled, trying to leave me high and dry. You dinosaurs are taking up space on my schedule and I don't like it." His expression and tone of voice turned almost smug. "This *is* a prison wing, Cody. I could recommend that you be kept here. Maybe you and your woman," he nodded at Sara, "could be assigned joining cells."

Sara couldn't resist a small smile. Cody's emotionless expression, as if carved in stone, to anyone else would likely appear calm. But telltale little signs let her know the only reason Parnell wasn't flat on his ass from a single pop to the jaw was Cody's discipline holding that in check.

Cody indicated Sara.

"Is this your doing, what happened to her? You seem to want Ms. Durrell's job an awful lot, you midlevel pencil pusher."

Parnell snickered.

"Don't be ridiculous. I don't need to resort to thuggery. Durrell is here as a result of her own inappropriate actions."

Sara said, "Boys, boys. You're talking about me like I'm not here."

Parnell ignored her.

He said to Cody, "You're pushing me hard, Cody. You and Durrell have been having your own inappropriate relationship on agency time. I'm only following agency protocol."

"Take it up with the president," said Cody. "Durrell is my liaison but he's the man I report to. His directive to me is clear and simple: get Vetrov. You don't intend to get in the way of that, do you, Jared?"

Parnell looked like he wanted to say something nasty. He growled his displeasure and cleared his throat.

"Okay, you're the miracle worker so for now I let you

slide. But I'm still overseeing the unit even if it is tempo-rary. My office will provide you with intel on Vetrov as it comes in. And if you feel like screwing up and making a few big mistakes, why, go right ahead. I'll be tracking from the wings to take you down. I don't like dinosaurs."

"Fair enough," said Cody, and he added to Sara, "I'll do what I can."

With that, he walked out.

Left alone in the room with Sara, Parnell crossed to the television. From his pocket he drew what appeared to be a pen. He pressed the tip against the corner of the TV screen. A sharp *crack!* reverberated through the room. The "pen" was an emergency services glass breaker, designed to shatter an automobile window in order to rescue a trapped driver or passenger. Applied to a televi-sion screen, it turned the screen into a spider-webbed sheet of black.

"Oops," Parnell said. "Looks like there's nothing on. No more contact for you with the outside world . . . until you cough up whatever sent you to that Thelma Justice rally."

Sara called him a dirty name. She closed her eye. Cody knew where to find the file on Aisha. She'd conveyed that during their coded conversation. Parnell continued to speak. Sara lowered the bed to its standard horizontal position. She concentrated on staring at the ceiling, allowing herself to yield to medicated detachment.

CHAPTER ELEVEN

THE PRESIDENT of the United States said, "Do you know who this is?"

Cody said, "I do have caller ID, sir. This be the boss man calling."

His cell screen had displayed an odd row of symbols that would've appeared meaningless to anyone else. But for Cody, it meant only one thing. One person.

"Very funny," said the president. "You okay, Jack?"

Martin Harwood's voice was filtered through who knew how many scramblers before completing the loop to Cody's cell. Cody was The President's Man, not only serving in that very *un*official capacity under Harwood, the incumbent Commander-in-Chief, but also for the POTUS's predecessor. The abiding personal, mutual respect—friendship was as good a word as any—that bonded Cody and the chief executive stemmed from Cody having personally risked his life, and taken the lives of others, to save the lives of President Harwood and the First Lady; a domestic terrorist action months earlier in Arizona.

Cody said, "I just touched down this morning, sir, but of course you know that. It's good to be back. First time in a while I've gone all day without anyone shooting at me. 'Course, the day's not over."

"I've been briefed on your mission. Welcome home, Cody. Russian authorities are cleaning up the mess you left behind and Russian-American relations are back on track."

"For now."

"You sound chipper."

"The blues singers call it smiling to keep from crying. Permission to speak freely, sir."

"Permission granted. You know you don't have to ask, not when it's between the two of us."

"Glad to hear it," said Cody. "Okay then, if I may speak plainly: what the hell's going on with Sara Durrell? She's filled me in on the basics."

The President interjected a sigh.

"Should have known. There's no stopping you two."

"I get the idea she's gotten herself into a mess."

"That's a fair assessment," said the president. "Disciplinary action resulting from unauthorized use of agency resources was bad enough but after the killing of members of Thelma Justice's security personnel, the so-called Furies of Harmony, and the involvement of some Middle East Princess, well, you're right." Another sigh traveled across the phone connection. "It's a real mess."

"I've scanned my news apps," said Cody. "I know who Thelma Justice is and about the rally she just held. But there's no mention of killings or a missing princess."

"No, and with any luck we'll be able to keep the lid on the whole damn thing until we have something substantial to offer up. It was crazy as hell, Jack. A hit team after this Princess Aisha, either trying to kill her or kidnap her. We're not even sure on that yet. And the young lady has disappeared. Eyewitnesses saw her being whisked away in a separate incident minutes after the killings. And get this. The killers used hi-tech crossbows to evade metal detectors, for crying out loud. The girl's family in Dubai isn't saying a thing."

"Okay," said Cody, "the media blackout is in effect. But . . ." He cocked an eyebrow. "That's it? That's what put Sara in hospital lockdown? What's up with this Parnell guy? He's leaning on Sara too damn hard. She's a good soldier."

"I know that," said the president, "and you know that I'm personally fond of Ms. Durrell. But I wouldn't be the first sitting president to have his entire political agenda sidetracked thanks to mucking about with interagency turf wars in the intelligence community."

"I keep forgetting, sir. You are a politician."

"Do try to remember that," said Harwood with tongue in cheek. "And consider. An Arabian Princess, Thelma Justice and three people dead. Between the price of oil and the whole situational ebb and flow of Mideast power plays, our posture for now is hoping forensics and the DOJ can find leads to start unraveling this. And, of course, it would be a great help if the princess decided to show up."

"And Parnell?"

"I said I'm fond of Sara, but protocol must be followed. I'll see what I can do. I may be a mere politician in the eyes of a fighting man but, dammit, I'm a damn good politician. Regarding the Durrell situation, I'll keep an eye on that. For now, that's the best I can do. And Jack, I don't want you getting involved in the business between Parnell and Sara. I want you to lay low. General Vetrov's present whereabouts is unknown but he'll surface soon enough. That's the nature of the beast. Those weren't the only nukes he has stashed away. We stopped his deal with the North Koreans but when he makes his next move, I want you rested and ready to take him on again. Vetrov remains your one and only mission, Cody. You did the world a favor, derailing that train shipment in the Urals. Now you need some down time. That's an order."

"Yes, sir."

That was good enough for the president. He ended the call without further comment.

Cody had stopped off at his townhouse. He rarely spent time there due to his missions keeping him on the move. The place was clean and spartan.

And undoubtedly under surveillance.

He spotted indications of minor disruptions that betrayed, to a careful eye, the planting of cameras and microphones in his quarters. He made a quick tour of his apartment and found four active, well-placed wires discernible only to a keen eye and knowing what to look for. There would be at least that many operating in short burst transmissions once their flash drives were full, in contrast to the standard broadcast surveillance devices.

From the window, he made a quick survey up and down the street fronting his address. A seven year old silver sedan sat at the opposite curb, halfway down the block. Someone sat at the steering wheel, their gender indeterminate from this distance. If this was Parnell's doing, it would likely be a subcontracted local asset in that car, Parnell being the politicking weasel sort who would cover his tracks if he could. He wanted to keep an eye on things.

With his thumbprint, Cody unlocked the tablet plugged into the dock near his television. He opened up his favorite live music streaming service to full volume. Every TV and Bluetooth device in his home erupted, blaring a tune—bouncy yet vulgar—belted out by a British songstress.

He stripped down and walked into his bathroom to scrub off the miles and stink in the shower. By the time he'd scoured himself raw with washcloth and pounding hot water and had turned off the shower head, his playlist had advanced to a pair of white rappers advising an unfair world to fornicate itself. Hardly his favored genre but when it came to numbing and distracting the snoops with something to listen to, he did appreciate having high end stereo speakers to blast vulgarity in any format. Next up on the list was a Texas hard rock/light metal group giving their all with growling lyrics and thrashing guitars.

Cody selected clothes for that night: black turtle-neck, khaki slacks, and a pair of coyote brown boots that matched the khakis. Before slipping into a twill jacket, he slid into the shoulder holster rig for his Beretta, tucking fresh magazines into the pouches at either side of the holster. From his gear, he snagged a multi-tool pliers set and a folding pocket knife, supplementing them with a high intensity mini flashlight.

A service entrance at the rear of his building and climbing a backyard fence distanced him every step of the way from whoever was sitting in that car across the street from his address. He stopped off at a mini market and picked up a pre-paid cell phone. It took a few moments to activate the phone before contacting the server to which Sara had uploaded a suite of software, downloadable to such burners. Just because the Agency had his personal phones monitored and traced didn't mean he had to go without programs that made his life and work easier. Before long he was descending into the DC Metro subway system, his senses peeled for the any indication of a tail. There was none.

When the underground train rolled in, Cody boarded and proceeded to ride. DC Metro is always busy; crowded but well-run. He switched cars twice before getting off the train with the other commuters. Once the subway was gone on its way, the steel shanks and padding of his boot soles cushioned his drop onto the tracks.

Parnell could easily access subway station security cams but there were no such lenses to spy upon Cody once he trudged along the tracks into the tunnel. He'd consulted his phone's updated GPS map to make certain he was making his way toward a discontinued "dead station." At about the halfway mark, he had to leap off of the tracks and press his back to the wall when a subway train came thundering through. The train's lighted windows went flying by.

Fifteen more minutes and he was again at street level, maneuvering through the approaching dusk toward Sara's apartment.

He must tread lightly in what he was about to do. There would be more than the third-rate contracted local asset presently keeping an eye and ear on his every movement. They likely intended him to spot that tail as a way of getting him to relax his guard. He must proceed with extreme caution.

Greb Vetrov was temporarily on the back burner. Cody intended to drop everything when new intel came in. Under normal circumstances, at this point he'd be indulging in serious R&R with Sara. Yeah, right. Normal, eh? Not this time. He would have to drop this —whatever *this* was—when the next piece of intel on the

Russian developed, which meant that in the matter of a princess, dead Furies, Thelma Justice and Sara Durrell, he must move fast.

Carol, the mother of his children, had been the love of his life and always would be.

Her best friend, Sara, was the most pragmatic and battle savvy woman Cody had ever known.

Sara was not a woman to waste her time. Why was she interested in Ms. Justice and Princess Aisha, and why was Parnell coming down on her so hard? Was it based on only his self-interest, or was there something else?

Cody knew only two things for certain.

He would learn the truth.

And nothing short of death would stop him.

CHAPTER TWELVE

SARA LIVED in an upscale residential neighborhood dominated by nearly identical six-unit apartment buildings. Cody circled the block, reconnoitering to determine if her address had been placed under surveillance.

The Agency had two cars posted at the opposite curb from her building at either end of the block. Their license plates were the tipoff.

They would be easy enough to avoid with the night as his ally. Cody reversed the jacket he wore, its black inner liner blending with the shadows of evening. With a pull of a zipper, the liner unfolded; more dark fabric down to knee level considerably altered his appearance. Glasses with thick, large frames further disguised his facial features. A tam cap from his pocket completed the transformation.

Another car showed up, wheeling in to the curb on Sara's side of the street, a half block up. Same car Cody had spotted across the street from his place. The driver remained behind the steering wheel, not getting out. Another sure tipoff.

Cody slipped between two of the apartment buildings, quiet as the shadows, into a common area/parking lot for the clustered apartment houses providing access for delivery and maintenance. He kept in the deepest shadows, scanning the parked cars back here for any indication of a surveillance team watching the rear entrance of Sara's building. He also noted placement of the security cameras for each building.

A brown Grumman Kurbmaster delivery truck sat backed near an adjacent building, its engine idling. The insignia on its side panel identified it as that of a well-known delivery service. Cody spotted the surveillance team huddled in the truck's rear. He became one with the deepest shadows, morphing into just a regular everyday guy strolling along in a perfectly natural manner. . . carefully avoiding the delivery van.

When he reached the far side of a neighboring apartment building two down from the one housing Sara's apartment, he went to work, withdrawing a slender, foot-long rod from his jacket compartment. He attached this to a wound loop of black nylon mountain-climbing rope rated to 660 pounds of carry weight; its 32-foot length opened easily. He snapped a coupling link into the base of the steel rod. The press of a button sprung three poly-carbonate claws from their recessed housings. Moving further along, he located a raised fire escape.

A toss of the grappling hook. It caught, whereupon he scaled the thirty feet, thanks to upper body strength and the traction of his boots against the building wall, to the bottom rung of the fire escape. When he'd gained his footing on its bottom rung, he re-wound his rope back into its compact bundle, returning it to its hidden pocket that also concealed the spring-clawed grapnel kit.

He continued up the fire escape, pausing at rooftop level.

Activating his burner phone's camera and external microphone, he swept the night sky with its lens while also activating the drone detection software he'd downloaded, an app designed to pick up what his naked eye could not see along with ultra-low frequency motor sounds that his natural hearing couldn't detect.

The scan revealed a drone active above Sara's building. It would be operated from one of those surveillance cars out front or the van in the rear. It wasn't likely to have camera power strong enough to pick him up on the roof of this building two whole buildings away. The drone was hovering low, its aerial access focused on that building's front and rear entrances.

Cody advanced across the roof of this building, making sure to keep air conditioning vents and catwalks between himself and the drone just in case. A quick glance through the cell's camera revealed the drone remaining stationary, hovering in place above Sara's apartment building. He brought the grapnel hook-up kit into play again, swinging to the next building's fire escape and making the short, quick climb to its rooftop.

He neared Sara's building, getting a better fix on the drone. It was the size of two hands pressed together at the wrists. The buzz of its propellers carried faintly. He could disable the damn thing with a gunshot from the Beretta but such destruction of the robot would only serve to inform the surveillance team that something was wrong. The only real threat from the drone was if it did catch him reaching that rooftop where he had intended to gain entrance via the roof access door.

He now searched the gloom instead for a point to swing across that would place him near the fire escape that clung to the side of that apartment complex. He found a point, unfurled the hook and swung across the gap separating the buildings. Rather than climbing up, he rappelled laterally to gain his footing on the fire escape where it ran beneath the window of a lighted corridor lined with apartment doors. He reeled in his climbing cord, dislodging its hook.

The window would be wired to go off if opened; a simple key lock mechanism independent from the panic bar that would trigger a fire alarm. Entry required a few minutes with his lock pick kit. Cody undid the locking mechanism and raised the window without activating the press-down alarm of the Outside Access Device.

Then he was inside.

Few—in this case, no one—would expect someone to reach this floor of the building by way of the fire escape, especially when its bottom rung was thirty feet off the ground and the window had been rigged to sound an alarm.

He slipped the tam cap and coke bottle glasses into a jacket pocket, scanning the hallway for security cameras. He came up blank. With their eyes on the front and back entrances of the building and a drone hovering overhead, those keeping an eye on Sara's domicile had deemed their efforts sufficient.

He advanced cautiously along the hallway. The door to Sara's apartment was slightly ajar.

What the hell?

He edged close up to the doorjamb, peering through the crack. Without opening the door further, the only view afforded through the crack was of a blank opposite wall of the foyer just inside the doorway. He heard the click of high heels and papers being rustled.

Given Parnell's hostility toward Sara Durrell, Cody

didn't think the guy would find a female agent "professional enough" for a job like this. And would an agency asset be tossing an apartment in clicking heels?

He moved silently away from the door, following Sara's directions that led him to where she, during their coded conversation at the hospital, had communicated to him where her files and info on Princess Aisha were stashed. Two doors down from her apartment and there it was, the air vent in the ceiling he was looking for. She'd confided in him once before that this was her "secret hiding place"; at the hospital, she'd indicated this was the place to look.

The cover was a diffuser style, four squares of angled metal designed to direct air flow, the middle square an aluminum pyramid.

He reached up with his closed grapnel hook, running it in a small circle around the diffuser's slots. The magnetic tip of the hook emitted a slight *click!* The flash drive adhering to it immediately loosened. Cody brought down the drive: a common brand of portable jump drive, capable of holding 64 gigabytes of information. Slender and light. Easy to conceal as those old-style tubes of microfilm used to be. Couldn't be read without a device, but he could solve that by simply using any tablet.

He pocketed the flash drive. Slowly, stealthily, he backtracked to Sara's apartment. The door remained open a crack as before. Cody used two knuckles to rap gently on the door.

A startled surge of response from inside.

Sudden movement. The lights went off. The shuffle of sheets of paper dropping to the floor. Those clicking high heels withdrew deeper into the apartment.

Cody did not draw his pistol but did let his fingertips hover close to it. He entered the apartment, no longer a silhouetted target against the hallway light. The person cornered in here either wasn't dangerous or wasn't much skilled with a firearm or they'd have already opened fire on him. He drew a pencil flashlight from his pocket. Its beam probed the apartment's dark interior.

Her shadowy silhouette was caught against the curtains in the little flashlight's narrow beam.

She held a small caliber, a lady's gun, aimed squarely at his chest. Had he come in with his Beretta drawn, she might well have opened fire. He'd been ready for that and was relieved it hadn't gone down that way. He switched on a table lamp, flooding Sara's apartment with a warm glow.

He took a step forward and lifted his hands, displaying his empty palms.

Cody said, "Don't shoot. I'm on your side."

CHAPTER THIRTEEN

SHE WAS RICHLY TANNED. Early thirties. Dark hair, full lips. Hazel eyes were clear, intelligent, almond shaped; long black lashes curving like wings. Smartly dressed. Suit and slacks conformed to healthy curves and long legs. A purse over her shoulder, its mouth open. The pages he'd heard her drop earlier had either been replaced wherever she found them or were in her purse.

She thumbed back her pistol's hammer.

"How do you know whose side I'm on?"

Cody took another step closer, casual as hell.

"That little pea shooter is not agency issue. You're not with the people who were after me."

"And who are you exactly?"

Cody took one step closer and plucked the pistol from her grasp. It almost disappeared in his fist. A tiny .25, made by Beretta. He popped out the magazine and racked the slide. No bullet ejected from the breech. He put the magazine back into the gun, flicked on the safety and made a judgment call. He handed the pistol back to her, butt-first.

"Name's Jack Cody. Who are you?"

She frowned down at the gun in her hand, then up at him.

"You trust me with the gun?"

"I can take it back before you flick off the safety," said Cody. "Again, who are you?"

She deposited the pistol into her purse.

"Tiff," she said. "Tiff Butler." Pause. She cleared her throat. "It seems we have a mutual interest in Ms. Durrell? "

Cody shrugged.

"I'm just checking in on my girlfriend's place. What's your excuse? "

She nibbled her lower lip between her healthy white teeth, continuing to take his measure with those intelligent eyes.

"I'm a journalist," she said, choosing her words carefully. "Don't ask me who I work for because I can't tell you that."

"And you're hot on the trail of a big story right here in Sara's home?"

A trace of skepticism to keep her off guard because she was an unknown. But whatever and whoever the lady was, eye contact and her steady demeanor clearly marked her as a cool one. Cody's first reaction was positive but cautious.

She said, "I'm trying to trace something that happened at the Thelma Justice event. Your girlfriend was involved. "

Cody said with a straight face, "I haven't heard anything about that."

"If you're lying," she said, "please stop. I was in the crowd at the Order of World Harmony convention. I saw Ms. Durrell open a man's arm up with a knife. She was protecting Princess Aisha, a visiting guest of the Order who happens to be the daughter of a wealthy Middle Eastern mucky-muck."

Cody pursed his lips. He glanced around the apartment. Tiff was glib with her answer. He wanted to hear more.

He said, "How about we go somewhere and talk this out? I spotted a little restaurant a few blocks down. "

"Sounds divine," she replied with a straight face of her own. "What about those enemies you mentioned?"

"They're watching this place. We'll be someplace else."

"Then lead on," she said without hesitation. "By the way, where is your girlfriend? "

"I think you know."

They used the apartment house stairs without further comment, Tiff as sure-footed as a mountain goat in her high heels. When they reached the building's ground floor, Cody again donned the cap and thick-lensed glasses, additionally inserting cotton in his cheeks to add an estimated twenty pounds to his facial appearance.

Tiff observed this, her curiosity mingled with mild amusement.

When they left the building through the lobby's main entrance, Cody kept his head hunched down between his shoulders so he would appear short alongside the woman who now seemed to tower over him by a head. Arm in arm, they crossed the sidewalk, passing by one of the agency sedans, Cody watching for any expression of recognition from within the vehicle. The tinted windows at night were impossible to peer through, but the lack of movement or sound from within the car indicated that his disguise was working.

———

THE RESTAURANT WAS A TWO-BLOCK STROLL. Traffic was more prevalent along a well-lit avenue. There were others out and about, walking in the Washington DC nightlife.

Cody didn't straighten to his full height or remove the accouterments of his disguise until they reached the place. A hostess guided them to a table, after which he visited the washroom to undo his disguise, reversing his jacket again to its twill normal and again pocketing the glasses and cap. When he returned to their booth, Tiff was visibly impressed by the transformation of his appearance.

"Wow. You are something, mister whoever you are."

"Wow," he repeated. "Is that reporter talk?"

She arched an eyebrow.

"I sort of want to like you, Cody. Are you going to make that difficult?"

"You said something about being a journalist."

"I also said something about not being able to tell you who I work for."

"Tell me anyway."

She was rescued by the arrival of their waitress. Tiff ordered a salad and green tea. Cody ordered a Coke and the burger he'd been thinking about.

When they were alone again, Tiff said, "I'm more comfortable being the one who asks the questions."

"You were in my girlfriend's apartment. Let's talk about that."

She looked around. The clinking of glasses and silverware and polite conversation from nearby tables drifted through the air. The place wasn't busy. It was a slow night.

She said, "Those enemies of yours, could they have followed us here?"

"I'd know it if they had. I'll know if they do. What were you looking for in Sara's? What did you find?" When she said nothing, he pressed with, "Tell me about this Princess Aisha. Why is she important?"

He wanted to know what she was willing to divulge even though the flash drive he'd concealed would likely provide much information. But he needed a solid something from this woman to better determine her role in these goings-on. If she were simply a journalist, then he was a seeing eye dog.

Tiff said, "Something about an ancient artifact the princess is said to have in her possession as a gift to Ms. Justice and the Order. There are rumors—"

"No facts?"

"Just rumors," said Tiff almost nonchalantly, and she began to say more.

"I'm short on time," said Cody.

He reached across the table and snagged the purse she'd set down beside her on the booth's bench seat. He tipped the purse upside down and its contents emptied onto the center of the table.

Tiff said, "Hey!"

The pistol made too small a *clunk* on the tabletop to draw anyone's attention. Besides the .25, the purse held only her phone, a pack of cigarettes and the usual stuff. He unsnapped her wallet and took a look at her driver's license, holding it up to compare the face across from him with its laminated likeness. She was who she said she was. He memorized her midtown address.

Cody said, "I heard you rustling papers. Where are they?"

Her mouth was a tight line. Intelligent eyes, not at all pleased, stared furious daggers at him.

"Those papers went back where I found them," she replied in a brittle voice. "I forget what they were. Nothing important. Nothing related to what I'm looking for. I'm not a thief."

"Maybe not but you know about Sara. Stop playing dumb. Nothing about you fits the part."

"Well that's a left-handed complement if I ever heard one."

"I said stop it," he said. How did you know it was Sara Durrell you saw with the princess?"

Tiff again glanced around to make sure they were unobserved. She went about gathering up her items on the table, replacing them in her purse except for her phone.

"I was in the right place at the right time." She scrolled through her phone's gallery. "I was browsing one of the book booths when it happened."

She angled the phone so Cody could view a photograph of Sara, an impromptu action shot rendered in HD clarity on the smart phone's screen: Sara Durrell wielding a razor sharp blade against a burly man in a baseball cap. The photograph was blurred in the swift and violent instant of the snapped shot.

Tiff's index finger brushed across the screen, revealing the next photograph. In this one, blood was visible from a deep wound in the man's arm.

Cody brought his index finger into play, swiping through a half-dozen sequenced photos depicting Sara engaged in a ballet of violence before being dropped to the ground by a savage blow that caught her by surprise. Cody studied the features of the second man who had caught her with that sucker punch and he felt a tightening of the spirit, déjà vu of what he'd experienced right after losing Carol and the kids to that terrorist bomb. . . those things again bubbled to the surface as he studied the images of the brutal pummeling that had put the woman he loved in the hospital.

He memorized her assailant's Arab features, height and weight, everything about him available from studying a photograph on a smart phone. The son of a bitch had done a good job of trying to disguise himself with mirrored shades and a reversed baseball cap, and his jacket was loose, all the better to conceal his physical stature.

"Any idea who these guys are?"

"I was hoping you'd know."

Cody said nothing. He withdrew his loaded burner and tapped a button on its smart screen. Tiff observed this with a trace of alarm.

"What are you doing?"

The smart device commenced cloning her phone's digital memory.

"Relax. I'm drawing those images off your cell."

"So your name's Cody. You can dodge professionals who are looking for you. You're a survivor. That's an impressive and dangerous combination. Who do *you* work for, Mr. Cody?"

"Forget that journalist noise," he said. "You're into some heavy duty trouble, lady. If you're on the wrong side of the fence, forget it. You're already done for because now I'm part of the picture."

"Is that so?"

"Yeah, that's so. I need to know who you are, Tiff Butler. I need pedigree. Who you represent, what you know, and I want that now."

She replaced her phone in her purse.

"I'm freelance. "

"Is that the truth? Nothing in your purse indicates press credentials."

"Why should I advertise? Yes, it's the truth."

"Why did it take me so long to get that out of you? "

"Because we keep being interrupted. "

She spoke having seen the waitress returning with their orders. The server delivered and departed. Cody began salivating just looking at the sizzling hamburger and fries on the plate before him.

The more he learned from and about this mystery woman sitting across from him, the stronger was his hunch that she could provide the next link in the chain that would take him closer to Princess Aisha, who seemed to be the key to Sara's predicament.

As his fingers closed around the burger bun and he opened his mouth for that first long-anticipated bite, Cody's peripheral vision registered a trio of hardcases shouldering their way into the restaurant. Big, ugly guys who couldn't have worn more black if they'd been dipped in coal dust. Their jackets were open and from the way those jackets bulged, these guys were heeled with serious firepower.

They paused for a moment just inside the entrance, surveying the half-filled eatery. Then they started toward Cody and Tiff.

Cody asked her, "Friends or foes?"

Tiff's tan had turned instantly pale, her eyes flaring wide. She seemed unable to speak.

The point man of the three was glaring daggers at her, reaching under his jacket, his men doing the same.

That made it clear enough.

Enemies.

And they were out for blood.

CHAPTER FOURTEEN

THE POINT MAN'S gun was halfway drawn.

Cody hurled his plate at the guy. The uneaten hamburger went flying in one direction, the fries in another, while the edge of the plate, like a porcelain frisbee, connected with the front man's forehead with enough force to knock the guy backwards into the other two men. Not much in terms of dissuasion but it gave the trio pause enough for Cody to seize Tiff Butler's wrist.

They burst from the booth, Cody pawing for his Beretta.

The restaurant had one entrance for its customers. There would be an exit through the kitchen, a storehouse of weaponry—hot surfaces, boiling oil, sharp objects—but there would also be kitchen staff and waitresses who could be caught in a crossfire. The last thing Cody wanted was for bullets to catch innocent citizens. Witnessing the abrupt arrival of the three men, urban-savvy patrons were already responding to the impending violence, men and women flinging themselves beneath tables, hugging the floor.

Cody led Tiff to a close-by waitress station, pushing her down behind it for cover. The intruders opened fire. Ice water pitchers exploded atop the waitress station.

One gunman stepped out by a booth under the window. Cody cut loose. He ripped two shots into the assailant's legs, one a glancing wound that sliced out a third of an inch of calf skin and muscle, the second striking him in the patella, obliterating the heavy knobbed end of his femur resting behind the kneecap. The gunman let out an agonized cry and crashed to the carpet, his torso smashing a wooden chair on the way down.

Cody bolted from Tiff who remained huddled below and behind the waitress station. He angled away from her, drawing the attention of the gunmen, giving him a clear shot at the plate-battered front man. That guy was in the process of tracking his piece on Cody. The Beretta barked twice, pitching the hardcase into a brick pillar that bordered the restaurant's glass entryway. The gunman slumped against the pillar and door frame, clutching his chest where Cody's rounds had struck.

Cody had hit his target, but the guy was wearing body armor! Cody upended a table, crouching behind and twisting it around for concealment, not cover. The third shooter's bullets splintered the heavy table, penetrating far too close for comfort. The man on the floor had sighted on Cody and opened fire, cranking the trigger on his auto pistol. But in agony from his wounds, his aim was way off. Cody surged to his full height and took a running charge at and dived through the restaurant's plate glass window. The glass flexed for a brief instant and he wondered if he'd made a big mistake but the glass gave, shattering under his weight and force. He landed on the sidewalk outside, thus drawing fire from any civilians inside.

Landing prone, he glanced up and down the street.

No one was out for a nighttime walk. Lights were on in brownstone flats along the block. The first calls to 911 were likely being made right now. He needed to take care of this situation promptly and get Tiff and himself the hell away from there.

Through the shattered window, he heard one of the gunmen rattle off a command. He couldn't quite hear the words but it sounded like a romance language, possibly Italian. The front doors of the restaurant remained closed, meaning enemy contact would next come from around a corner of the establishment.

Two gunshots barked from somewhere inside, sounding like the snap-snap of Tiff's .25.

Cody hustled to the nearest corner, catching one of them with a powerful shoulder tackle that folded the other man in half, lifting the guy off his feet and plowing him into a utility pole.

The sudden stop against that unyielding pole was a stunning blow to Cody's left shoulder, nearly spinning him out into the side street. He heard the other's bone crack with the impact. He backed away. The stunned gunman dropped to all fours on the pavement at the curb. Cody whipped the muzzle of the Beretta across the man's jaw. The front sight and barrel laid open skin down to pink bone from under an ear to the tip of his chin. The foreigner, senseless and off balance, collapsed to the ground.

The third guy—the one wearing body armor—now fully recovered, chose that moment to emerge from the restaurant's front entrance behind Cody. He took aim at

Cody's back, smug in the knowledge that even if his presence was discovered by his target, his lightweight body armor protected him.

Some sixth sense warned Cody. He spun around.

Two gunshots rang out. The gunman dropped with two tiny .25 caliber bullets drilled into the back of his brain.

Cody started to thank Tiff when that sixth sense again tugged his attention around. The gunman he'd left semi-conscious by the pole, the one he intended to interrogate, was making a break for it by dodging between cars parked along the curb. Cody shot him in the right hip.

A colorful Italian curse cinched the guy's nationality. He slammed against the front fender of a sedan, dropping out of sight when he saw Cody advancing on him. A magazine clattered onto the asphalt, another box could be heard getting slapped into place.

Cody came to a halt in front of the grille of an SUV.

A thickly accented voice challenged from its other side, "You want some more, *signor?* " and two bullets punched through the hood of the SUV.

Cody drew back. He made out the man's legs and a foot through the clearance of the heavy vehicle. The Beretta spoke. Another Italian curse. But still the guy didn't fall. Cody sprang to his feet, seeing through the SUV's windows that the man was remaining upright now only by holding onto the SUV's roof rails. When Cody walked around the SUV and came toward him, the tough as nails, resilient dude started to swing his pistol up. Cody snatched hold of the guy's forearm, twisting it behind the man's back until he dropped his gun. This one needed to be quieted down so he could be interrogated. Cody bounced the gunman's face off the

SUVs side mirror. The metal piping that held the mirror bent violently against the door. Then Cody slammed the man's face into the SUV's side window. The safety glass cracked under the forceful impact but held, the window's spider webbing red from blood seeping into the fissures.

Cody growled, "Who are you, dammit? Give it up. You don't have to die. Talk to me."

The damn guy twisted with enough sideways force to dislodge himself from Cody's hold.

"*Morituri te saluant!* " he burbled through broken teeth and shredded lips.

He surged mightily, making a last ditch reach for his pistol on the ground. Cody grimaced and drove the gunman forehead-first through the SUV's cracked window, its sharded glass driving into the Italian's wind-pipe. The man went limp.

Cody released him, letting the dead man drop into a widening pool of his own blood that looked like spilt black oil under the streetlights.

Tiff approached on the run, her high heels clicking, the diminutive .25 in her fist.

Cody said, "Careful. There's a third one still around."

"He's long gone," she replied. "I finished him inside before he could do any more damage."

That explained the two gunshots he'd heard from inside the restaurant.

He said, "You give a good accounting of yourself."

He reloaded and holstered the Beretta, then scooped up the dead man's piece. Child's play, separating the slide and the frame of the gun. He tossed the magazine into a curbside storm grate. Tiff slid the .25 into her purse.

Sirens could be heard piercing the night, approaching double time from several directions. Little doubt those Agency stakeout vehicles from around Sara's would also be responding.

Tiff said, "We've got to scram and fast."

Cody withdrew his burner phone.

"Need a mo."

He thumbed on the flash for his phone's camera and took pictures of the dead man's fingerprints and then of the guy's ear, another good means of identification if photos of the fingerprints didn't come out clear enough.

Then he seized Tiff by her wrist and led her at a fast clip to a street that intersected this one. From there, he spotted a causeway between two dark buildings. They disappeared into shadow, she hustling along in pumps, and reached where the causeway fed onto an alley. Cody guided them across the alley and through a courtyard shrouded in gloom.

Cody hesitated and Tiff sensed something.

"What is it?"

"I'm processing," he told her. "You just killed two men."

"So? A good accounting of myself. They were out to kill us. What was I supposed to do? "

"You could have tried doing what I did. Do your best to get information first. Make it less difficult for me to tag who those guys were. "

"Sorry for not wanting to die," she said tartly, "but the one you left alive inside was still armed and ready to kill. And when I came outside, that bastard wearing body armor was up again and ready to shoot you. I did save your life, Cody. "

"That," he conceded, "is a fact. Much obliged. Those boys spoke Italian. Mean anything to you?"

"Not a damn thing," she said. "I'm as clueless as you

are about those three. Now can we please get the hell gone?"

Headlights from the street were approaching the alley.

By unspoken mutual consent, they hurried to conceal themselves behind a row of lidded trash containers and a dumpster. Seconds later, one of Parnell's Agency sedans turned into the alley, its headlights gliding across the trash cans and dumpster.

The car crawled slowly past.

Tires crunched to a rubbery halt. The driver doused the headlights. The passenger side front door opened and a man debarked, pistol drawn. Cody couldn't recall his name but he recognized him in the dome light from inside the car. A low rung company man.

CIA guys working on American soil . . .

Cody whispered close to Tiff's ear, "I'll be right back."

He left her side, easing along a shadowed wall to within several feet of the car without being detected.

A male voice from inside the car said, "See anything?"

The outside man groused, "Hell, he's long gone. If it was him."

Police sirens kept drawing closer. No more than a block or two away.

"If it was Cody," the driver said, "Parnell's going to have our ass for losing him. Screw it. Come on. Let's get out of here. "

The one with the pistol scanned the alley one more time, his line of vision skittering across dumpster and trashcans. He exhaled a deep breath that could have been frustration or might have been relief. He returned to the car. As the sirens closed in, the driver floored the gas.

Rear tires squealed, spitting a plume of burnt rubber. Their traction caught and the Agency vehicle fired off down the alley. Another squeal of tires at the far end and they were gone.

And so was Tiff.

She wasn't where he'd left her. She was nowhere in sight. She'd seen her chance to extract herself from the situation and she'd taken it. Yeah, real gone. The excitement and the police presence remained centered in and in front of the restaurant. Back here in the alley, the silence of the urban night remained heavy and brooding.

Cody walked away, each step creating more distance between him and the carnage left behind. Along the way, he reversed his blood-spattered coat back to its long version, wiping specks of blood from his face and hands.

This roller coaster he'd been riding since his return to DC earlier that day had just turned *very* hot, *very* fast. Damn if he wasn't down the rabbit hole. Okay. But where the hell was this rabbit hole taking him?

Sara Durrell in lockdown.

Government surveillance.

A missing Middle East princess.

Thelma Justice and her Order of World Harmony.

A hit team that conversed in Italian.

And now, Ms. Tiff Butler . . .

CHAPTER FIFTEEN

Jared Parnell was in full steam mode, ears hot and his practically nonstop nicotine hits off the vape pen not doing a damn thing to soothe his edgy nerves. He stalked down the hall at Bethesda toward Sara Durrell's room/cell with a determined stride.

But when he pushed on the door latch, it resisted. He'd assumed it to be unlocked since a uniformed soldier had been posted next to her door. The locked mechanism stopped Parnell cold, so abruptly that he walked right into the door panel with a noisy thump, his interrupted forward momentum popping a tendon along his forearm. He glared at the soldier as a way of preventing any sort of comment.

Parnell was too pissed off about what had brought him here to remember the passcode. With a snarl of irritation he brought up the numbered sequence on his phone and tapped it out on the lock's keypad. The door swung inward, soundlessly and with maddening slowness, accompanied by Sara's chuckle of amusement.

"Having a rough day, Jared? You need to be smarter than the door."

"My rough day started with your friend Cody's return," Parnell snarled. "I want to know where the hell he went off to after he left here."

"You've come to the wrong place, buddy, if you want that information. Or anything else, for that matter."

"Don't call me buddy. Where is he? "

Sara waggled a thumb at the single chair across the room.

"Maybe in my blind spot? It hurts to turn my head too far to look in that direction. "

"Listen, Durrell, I don't know who you think you are—"

"I'm a CIA analyst and coordinator," she said, "just like you. That is, until you got the bright idea to start playing game of thrones with our department and making every kind of trouble for good people who don't deserve it."

"Cody was in a firefight a short time ago. Happened a couple blocks from where you live."

Sara disciplined her emotions and features there in the bed. *Careful*, she reminded herself. Words carried consequence.

"Is that right?"

"That's right." He named the restaurant. "I had your building under surveillance. I knew Cody would show up there."

"Huh."

"What the hell's that supposed to mean?"

"Huh means huh. Why are you here questioning me, Jared? Why are you so down on Jack Cody?" She rattled the cuffs that shackled her to the bed frame. "I sure as hell haven't been anywhere. You made sure of that. I haven't seen Cody. Why are you here asking me about him? What's your game, Jared?"

"I'm taking our department into the 21st century." Parnell's eyes glittered with icy determination. "With you and Cody having your way it's been like a Wild West rodeo. No more. Cody's going down."

"Tell me what happened. Was he hurt?"

Parnell regarded her with distaste.

"You really care about the guy, don't you?"

"And are you sure it even was Cody?"

"I've seen security camera footage from the restaurant," said Parnell. "It was Cody. He left three men dead."

"That sounds like Jack. Did he show up at my apartment house?"

"No, apparently the shootout went down before he could get to your place. There's an all points alert out for him from the feds and D.C cops. He won't get far. Where is he, Durrell?"

"I told you I don't know. Who are the men he took down?"

"They haven't been identified yet. It's a fluid situation. And that is why you and I are having this conversation. You saw him and talked with him right in this room before I showed up today. What did you talk about?"

She nodded at the window casement.

"Don't your microphones work? He and I have been to that restaurant. They serve great coffee and breakfast for dinner if that's what you want."

Parnell thrust himself forward to tower above her restrained figure. His eyes glazed and his fists were clenched.

"Lying bitch," he snarled. "What did you tell him while he was here?"

She would not have flinched even if her arms weren't restrained. If her wrists were freed from the padded leather straps, she'd have met his surge with a closed fist just behind the jaw.

She simply said in a matter of fact voice, "I don't know what you're talking about. "

Parnell leaned in closer above her.

"Code. You spoke to each other in code. You and Cody weren't chattering about brainless old movies. You were communicating information to him using some personal code between you." He looked ready to strike her. He wanted to strike her. He said, "Durrell, you really should be more frightened of me. "

Sara wrinkled her nose.

"Would you mind stepping back? Those garbage cartridges you smoke make your breath bad enough to choke a dung beetle. "

The guard at the open doorway stepped into the room, his hand resting on the butt of his holstered pistol. He addressed Parnell.

"Sir, please maintain a safe distance from the prisoner. "

Parnell whirled on the young man.

"Mind your business, soldier. "

The guard, an E-4 no more than twenty, was not intimidated by the suit.

"Sir, the security of this prisoner is my business."

Sara did her best not to smile as Parnell drew away from her, the anger in his eyes and the thrust of his jaw only growing more pronounced. She observed him with a cold gaze from her good eye.

Parnell glared at the guard.

"Satisfied?"

"Yes, sir. Thank you, sir."

The guard returned to his post in the hallway. His hand no longer rested on his pistol. A point had been made. The door remained open.

Parnell said to Sara, "Three men dead. A shootout. Gone before my men showed up. Cody should have remained on the scene until they arrived. If he had to quit the scene, he should have reported in. It's another example of his cowboy mentality and the problems it can cause."

"Your only problem," Sara retorted, "is you can't keep up with Cody. Forget it, Jared. You don't stand a chance. He's Jack Cody, the president's man. You'll be history by the time this is over."

"I'm tracking that cowboy. He's going down hard."

Sara snickered.

"Sure you are. Sure he is. Tracking him? Right."

Parnell's lips drew tight into a bloodless line. You could tell he was reminding himself that everything said here was being digitally recorded. His eyes flicked to the cameras and microphones placed throughout the room.

He said, "So you want to go on the official record as stating you don't know where Cody is."

"I do," said Sara. "You've had me installed here since what happened to me at the Thelma Justice event. How the hell should I know anything about Cody after he left?"

"You think you're smart," sneered Parnell. "See how far it gets you. I'll be back, Durrell."

"I can't wait, Parnell."

He held eye contact with her, a laser duel between them that lasted several extended seconds as if that was supposed to impress or intimidate her. Then he turned about and left her alone, the door closing after him. When she was alone, Sara broke into a wide, self-satisfied cat-ate-the-canary smile. She didn't give a damn if one of the hidden cameras did catch and record it.

Parnell thought this restaurant shootout had prohibited Cody from reaching her apartment building. She knew Cody better than that and Jared Parnell should have known too. Nothing stopped Jack Cody from doing what he intended. She didn't know what caused the firefight but she was willing to bet it was somehow tied in with Princess Aisha.

Cody had been to her place. He'd retrieved the flash drive she'd hidden. He'd walk away from the firefight. He was on the loose and on the case.

Well, all right!

It didn't take long for her to learn what details had been released. Her TV that Parnell had damaged had not yet been replaced, but the young soldier at the door managed to locate a small transistor radio for her. He switched it on just as local news was reporting the firefight. Little information being released this soon after the incident. No names. The radio news report called it an attempted robbery by three armed men, none of whom survived. Two restaurant patrons, a man and a woman, resisted and the firefight commenced. The man was Cody. But who was the woman at the restaurant? Friend or foe?

Sara repressed a fleeting pang of jealousy.

It all had to do with Princess Aisha, Sara was certain of that. But who and what else was involved? Cody would determine the significance of that ancient artifact and would follow through. What did it all mean? How did it all tie in? Who was Parnell and what was he up to? Was he tied in with Thelma Justice and the Order of World Harmony?

Sara detested being cut off from the world, alone in

her hospital room. They'd confiscated her tablet and cell phone. She closed her eye. The doctor told her the eye problem was not serious and would return to normal before long. She tried to speed that process along by relaxing and clearing her mind of troubling thoughts. But it wasn't easy.

What a mess.

What a *deadly* mess.

What, Sara wondered, would happen next?

CHAPTER SIXTEEN

AFTER SHE PARKED the rental car, the nighttime silence of the hotel garage allowed Tiff Butler's thoughts to break through the mental barriers of disciplined restraint that had served her in driving here from the shooting scene. The madly surging adrenaline flow was beginning to stabilize. Thoughts now swarmed about in her brain like carrion flies on a carcass. She needed a cigarette to calm her nerves before making her report to Thelma.

Tiff had given up smoking years ago. She'd long kept a pack in her purse to prove to herself and the world just how strong she was to resist her once heavy habit. As one of Ms. Justice's ranking inner circle of disciples, smoking was a definite no-no. Screw that, Tiff told herself.

After her psyche-shredding encounter with the man called Cody, she needed a smoke and no damn mistake!

Oh, she'd handled herself well enough. Hell, she had the training to do so, didn't she? As a Fury of Harmony, head of its plainclothes division. Before joining The Order of World Harmony, Tiff Butler had worked before that in military intelligence and on the NYPD. As for putting a pair of bullets into the back of that man's head, at the time it had seemed a good way a good way of getting on Cody's good side. But by the time it all went down in and around that restaurant, Tiff had decided that the best thing to do was make herself scarce. She was now hoping that saving Cody's life hadn't been a mistake.

Once they'd made it into that alley, she'd seen her chance to drop out of the scene and she took it. And honestly she didn't regret saving Cody's life. From a purely objective heterosexual woman's point of view, that big guy was a damn fine specimen of manhood!

He thought she was investigating the action at the Justice event, the killing of those Furies and the missing princess. He would assume she was a journalist of some sort. She could hardly tell him she was a faithful follower of Thelma Justice. Her story that she was researching a book on Princess Aisha was in fact good cover for Thelma's organization to go about gaining useful information on the girl's situation.

And now here she was, about to make her report to Thelma. For the first time in years, hell yes Tiff needed a smoke!

She withdrew a cigarette from the pack in her purse. With trembling fingers she fumbled her lighter and it dropped from her fingers, the hot coil stinging her thigh. She snatched the fallen heating element, replacing it into its socket, cursing as ash fumbled over her lapels. The fabric instantly warped and melted. Beneath the slacks her skin was livid and tender. She fervently cursed an unladylike word.

Knuckles rapped on her side window.

"Tiff. "

It was Windy Duke.

Tiff tried not to act startled. But she was. She opened her door, grimacing as the cigarette dropped to the dark, oily pavement. She regarded the smeared burn on the leather of the interior.

She said with a sigh, "That's going to be a headache. "

"What happened? Did you get into the woman's apartment? You seem, uh, frazzled."

"I need to see Thelma."

"She's been worried. You were supposed to call as soon as you left Durrell's. Your lack of contact—"

"Give it a rest, Windy," Tiff heard herself snap. "Some heavy shit went down, okay? Three dead, okay? And I ran into this guy . . . Windy, we've got a new somebody to worry about and that's no lie. Thelma is not going to like this."

"Relax, Tiff. I'm on your side. "

Tiff took a deep breath. Bile rose in her throat. She winced at its acid taste.

"I'm trying. That's what the cigarette was going to be for. "

"Come on, " said Windy. Her manner softened, trying to sound inviting. "Nothing ever got easier by putting it off, right?" She held out her hand. "Let's get upstairs. Thelma is waiting. "

———

"REPORT," said Thelma.

Windy sat in an armchair off to the side, saying nothing, staring at the tablet screen in her lap. She would be recording the conversation, Tiff knew, to be transcribed and archived for future reference.

Tiff, seated across from Thelma, said, "I found

nothing in Sara Durrell's apartment. It was under surveillance, I'm not sure by who."

"That means we are on the right track," said Thelma. "We're not the only ones interested. Go on."

"A man named Cody showed up. A . . . formidable man, to put it mildly. Government agent? Something like that. I tried to bluff my way out by drawing a gun. He took the gun away and handed it back to me. Said he's Sara Durrell's boyfriend. He wore a disguise to slip through the surveillance guys. An impressive fellow. Asked a whole lot of questions and didn't get much from me. I had to throw him a bone so I told him I was investigating what happened at your rally, the killing of those Furies. He thinks I'm a journalist. I brought up Aisha to see if I could learn what he knows. Before that could happen we were attacked in a restaurant by a hit team."

Thelma arched an eyebrow.

"He took you to dinner?"

"We want information, right? It seemed a direct way to go about getting it."

Thelma considered this for several seconds, then nodded.

"Continue."

Tiff proceeded to deliver a concise account of the firefight including the spoken Italian and the fact that she'd killed a man to save Jack Cody's life.

Thelma frowned.

"Let us hope that was not a mistake."

"Didn't think you'd like it much after I thought about it," Tiff admitted, "but by then it was too late and it seemed like a good idea at the time. I doubt Cody knows what to make of me at this point. I decided the prudent course was withdrawal so here I am.

"You decided right," Thelma nodded. "Windy, see to it that this Jack Cody is thoroughly researched."

"Yes, ma'am," Windy said without lifting her eyes from her tablet screen.

Tiff had decided not to tell Thelma that Cody had taken from her phone the picture's of Sara's attackers. One screw-up—not killing Cody when she'd had a chance—was bad enough.

Thelma said, "This fellow Cody is a complication I had not expected."

Tiff plunged ahead after some hesitation.

"He does have my name and address."

"That is why I want you to drop off their radar," said Thelma. "Everything is in flux since the disappearance—the abduction—of the princess. I've lost faithful Furies to violence and by losing the princess we've lost—for now—whatever valuable artifact she was bringing as a gift. We ID'ed the Durrell woman from the ambulance company records after she was attacked. My take away is she had just connected with Aisha when it happened. Durrell knows as little or much as we do. Less, I'd say. For right now, that makes this Cody the wild card."

"You can say that again," agreed Tiff, "and those I-tye gun boys have still got me scratching my head."

"It adds up to four interested parties who seem to want Princess Aisha for themselves," said Thelma. "There's us and, unless she's gone missing under her free will, there's the group that struck at the reception with their damn crossbows for crying out loud. That's the same bunch that hit you and this Cody at the restaurant. If I'm right, now they're hot on the trail to find her. High-tech crossbows is too Old World meets New for it to be anything else so I'm hanging that on your Italian speakers until we learn different. Then there's the US government. We know Sara Durrell holds an administrative position highly placed in the Central Intelligence Agency, thanks to Windy's research. And let's not forget Aisha's brother and family back in Dubai . . . or here in Washington, DC for that matter. One group killed to get their hands on her at the reception but she gave them the slip but fell into her brother's hands shortly after she met the Durrell woman."

Tiff said, "Are you sure this is the time for me to drop out of sight? Seems like things are about to get very hot around here. Things already have, haven't they? Handling the hot trouble, that's always been my job."

"But now Cody's in the mix," said Thelma. "We'll have his pedigree soon enough. But you obviously consider him a man of extreme competence. That's good enough for me. You're going underground, Tiff. Paris, I think. Yes, Paris. Our presence is well established there and you can continue to research the princess."

"As you wish," said Tiff.

Windy closed and set aside her tablet. She rose to escort Tiff out of the room.

Some, those not in the know, might have expected a hug of affection to pass between Ms. Justice and the woman who was basically one of her top enforcers. But no, their association was always cordial but it was Thelma's militantly feminist philosophies that drew and kept Tiff Butler in her service. The woman up close was too unreadable, too much of a cold fish for even Tiff's trained investigative skills to penetrate.

Thelma Justice was a force of nature, a power onto herself.

The "force of nature" leaned back against the plush cushions of her couch and considered what she'd just heard. Cody. Who the hell was Cody? Windy would find out in short order. Her assistant's modest, unassuming nature belied a demon of online research. Before that, though, Thelma would have Windy fix her another strong shot of vodka.

Thelma heard Tiff being politely shown out. Then a new voice as another was shown in. A male voice. A Russian accent. Windy appeared in the doorway.

"Ma'am, you have a visitor."

Thelma felt her heart beat faster.

"Show him in, Windy. That will be all."

"Yes, ma'am."

Windy withdrew.

Greb Vetrov strode in, pausing in the doorway for the intended dramatic effect. Thelma Justice was already on her feet.

"Darling!" she cried with the ecstasy of a teenage girl. "Welcome home!"

And she ran into her lover's arms.

CHAPTER SEVENTEEN

GENTLEMEN CENTRAL WAS a two-story structure marked by a flashing red and yellow neon sign flaring across a sidewalk busy even at this late hour. The joint was sandwiched in between a sex toys novelty shop and a more sedate structure that, in this edgy urban neighborhood, could well have been a brothel.

A guy stood on the sidewalk in front of the club, raising his voice above the blaring music spilling out from the doorway behind him, shouting at the dense flow of passersby.

"In here, gentlemen! Right this way! The prettiest girls in DC! Lap dances! Cheap drinks!" When Cody passed him on his way in, the man said, "Excellent choice, sir, and have a good—"

The rest was lost beneath the assault on Cody's senses as he stepped across the threshold into the club. The floor and walls of the place shuddered to recorded rock music that vied in decibel level with the inebriated hooting and hollering of drunken "gentlemen."

On small, round stages, placed strategically

throughout the club, shapely young women danced suggestively beneath baby pink stage lights. The over-amped atmosphere of rowdy patrons and the slam-bang music combined to make it seem to Cody as if there was not enough oxygen in there. He brought an elbow into play and nudged his way through to the impressive oak bar that ran the length of the club. The bar was lined three deep with patrons.

Cody stood at one end of the bar and beckoned a harried-looking bartender who wore a spotless white shirt and black bow tie. The bartender sidled over to him.

"Yes sir, what'll it be?"

He had to shout over the surrounding racket. Cody leaned across the bar, getting jostled from both sides.

"I want Barney Lund."

"Don't know him," the bartender said promptly, and turned his back on Cody to attend to a cluster of raucous servicemen, some of whom had their arms around provocatively dressed "working girls" present to help patrons get drunk while the girls drank watered-down cocktails before offering favors for a price with the house taking a cut of the action.

It was that sort of place.

"I'll find him myself," Cody said to himself.

There was a beaded curtain to one side of the bar, and he commenced elbowing his way in that direction. An archway led to a narrow stairway to the building's second level. Cody stepped through the archway and, with a last glance over his shoulder in the barman's direction, he saw the bartender pausing in his work to speak hurriedly into a house phone next to his cash register, his eyes on Cody as he spoke.

Cody climbed the stairs, two at a time, to a well-lighted landing. A carpeted hallway, lined with doors, stretched in either direction from the landing. A pair of musclebound guys, wearing black T-shirts and matching slacks, stood before the first door to the right.

Each of these guys had obviously spent more than a little time working out and likely an equal amount of time dishing out pain to misbehaving patrons. Their overdeveloped muscles bulged beneath their T-shirts. One of them was just thumbing off his cell phone and sliding it into a back pocket. There was no doubt he had just finished speaking with the bartender.

He glowered at Cody.

"What do you want?"

It was not a friendly question. Shoulder to shoulder, they blocked Cody's approach to the door behind them. The second one sneered as if dealing with errant customers was nothing new.

"No girls up here, dude. Get your ass back downstairs."

"I don't want a girl," said Cody. "I want to see Barney."

"No Barney up here," the first one snarled. "Get your ass lost or we'll kick it out of here."

"Funny," said Cody. "Barney Lund happens to own this den of iniquity."

The one on the left frowned.

"Den of what?"

"I said take me to him," Cody said quietly, "or I'll take myself."

The guy on the right said, "We'll take you, cowboy, out back and beat the crap out of you, that's what we'll do."

"Don't telegraph it," said Cody. "Bring it on."

They came at him in unison, the one on the right

bringing up his fists, which were adorned with brass knuckles. His partner swung a leather sap out and up, arcing it around toward Cody's head. Cody clamped both of the his hands like a vise around the wrist of the arm swinging the blackjack and shoved that wrist back so the sap sharply smacked the man between the eyes with enough force to knock him off his feet, breaking his nose. Cody then brought the man's arm down across his raised knee. The *crack!* of the arm breaking was unusually loud in the confines of the hallway. The man opened his mouth and shouted out his pain.

Using the guy's considerable bulk to block the swing that came at him from those brass knuckles, Cody released the broken arm. The other guy had momentarily lost his balance. Cody smashed this one's face into the wall. The man collapsed, sprawling across the carpet next to his companion, a thin trickle of blood oozing from one nostril of his broken nose. Their ragged breathing filled the corridor.

Cody turned when he sensed movement behind him.

Barney Lund had positioned his wheelchair in the doorway. He regarded the fallen men as he fired a cigarette from a Zippo lighter. Then he shifted his gaze to Cody through a cloud of exhaled smoke.

"Looks like I need to hire me some competent help. Hey, Jack."

"Hey, Barney."

Barney Lund, forty-something years old, with owl-like features, a balding pate and deep, knowing eyes that were magnified by the thick lenses of his glasses. He had the gruff, authoritative manner of a big man despite his diminutive stature in the wheelchair. Large-boned, salt-and-pepper bearded, he possessed an easy-going personal style that, Cody knew, would have remained unchanged in the presence of the Pope or a pimp.

Footfalls clumped up the stairway. Another pair of bouncers arrived. They took one look at the situation and threw themselves at Cody.

Barney raised a hand, halting them in mid-stride.

"Let him be," he commanded quietly. He indicated the fallen men. "Get these two out of here. They're fired. See that these bouncers bounce when you toss them out the alley door."

"Yes sir, Boss," both men chimed in unison like harmonizing parrots.

They each tossed one of the unconscious bouncers over a shoulder and trundled them away. Cody relaxed, stepping over to trade a firm handshake with the man in the wheelchair.

"Thanks, Barn. Sorry about the fuss."

Barney chuckled.

"Hey, it's not like bonehead goons aren't a dime a dozen in this town . . . and I'm including too many of those bought-off flunkies serving on the Hill." He back-wheeled his chair from the doorway. "Come on in, buddy. Help yourself to some coffee, if you dare."

The office appeared at first to be a hodgepodge of male disarray, but was in reality a utilization of every available space for stacks of books and plants. A tawny-colored pet ferret left its cage and came over to make a sniffing circle around Cody before returning to the cage, completely disinterested. Modern jazz filtered softly from unseen speakers. The office's most prominent feature was the enormous plate glass window that provided an ideal vantage point, a bird's-eye view of the crowded, raucous strip club interior below. The office was obviously sound-proofed, creating a strange effect like viewing a silent movie nightclub scene accompanied by soothing, relaxing jazz.

Barney scanned the carnal madhouse beyond the glass. He frowned, emitted a growl of displeasure, and picked up a phone beside a computer in a corner work area.

Cody saw the same busy bartender he'd spoken to moments earlier. The harried man picked up the house phone next to his cash register on what must have been its first ring. Cody turned to a coffeepot to draw himself a cup as Barney commenced barking orders into the phone like a military field commander.

"Those three soldier boys in front of you," he snapped at the bartender. "They're fixing to tussle with those homies next to them. I see it coming. Get some hostesses over there fast to level things off. And that jerk at table seventeen. I saw him pinching that lap dancer's titties just now and that's a goddamn no-no. See that he's bounced."

He didn't wait to listen to the chattering reply across the connection, which Cody could hear from across the room. Barney ended the call and set the phone aside. He wheeled around to face Cody.

Barney Lund had been struck by polio at age eight and wheelchair bound ever since. But this terrible illness and life in a wheelchair had in no way blunted Barney Lund's zest for life. It was much as when a blind person's system compensates with an increased awareness of the other senses.

Jack Cody was born into the economic upper middle class. Barney was from a far different background. His folks were live-in nanny and personal assistant to a rich family down the road from the Cody home in rural Maryland. Barney's parents would have been called a maid and a butler in earlier times. They lived in a small house behind their employers' and somehow Barney and Jack had become buddies around the age of ten.

One of their favorite pastimes had been taking hikes in the woods around where their families lived. Barney couldn't do any serious hiking, obviously, but with Jack pushing the wheelchair they'd make forays into the woods and have long conversations discussing girls and movies and girls and what they would become when they grew up and, of course, girls . . . until that time came when they began actually dating girls instead of just talking about them.

Now, the man in the wheelchair replenished his own coffee cup and regarded Cody over the rims of his Ben Franklin glasses that had slid to the tip of his nose. Taking a noisy, slurping sip of the bitter brew he'd always referred to as rocket fuel, Barney regarded Cody with an owlish gaze.

"I hear you're on the loose, Jack."

"More than on the loose, old buddy," said Cody with a growl. "I'm off mission. In the cold."

"Yeah, heard something about that too, now that you mention it." Barney casually indicated his PC. "I monitor the classified ops nets out of Langley and a few other places for recreation, the way the good old boys eavesdrop on the police band. You, Jack Cody, are their primary item of intense interest as we speak, to put it mildly. That's according to coded chatter which is reliable, oh, about 100% of the time."

After attending college, Barney had gone on to work professionally and with distinction in the field of psychology before dropping out, utterly disinterested in the "bullshit politics" of that profession, as he had informed Cody at the time. Blessed with an IQ in the genius range, Barney had gone on to teach himself computers, mastering them to such a degree that Cody had been instrumental in arranging a "working" visit for his best friend to the computer "shop" at the CIA HQ in Langley. In an idle, offhanded way, Barney, purely in observer status, had managed to isolate several glitches in the algorithms that had been driving the computer staff nuts. Following massive background checks, security clearances and the like, a process that had pushed Barney to being as grouchy and irascible as Cody had ever seen him, Barney Lund had not only fixed those computer glitches for the CIA but had gone on to completely overhaul and redesign a relay program's software designed to reroute encoded transmissions. Upon Barney's completion of the overhaul, after witnessing this astounding self-taught computer whiz in action, the powers that be had taken the unprecedented step of requesting that Barney Lund be permanently assigned to a civilian tech supervisory role.

The only roadblock: once his work was done, Barney had taken his fat paycheck and disappeared.

Cody said, "So what do you know about me that I don't know?"

"For starters," said Barney dryly, "given the tinderbox known as Middle East politics and everyone in the world gaming for a high stakes lock on their oil, they're afraid you could trigger World War III. And I am not indulging in idle hyperbole." Barney's gaze became dead serious. "Something about murders and shootouts here in DC and a missing princess from Dubai. I suppose you could conceivably know what you're doing."

"So you know about Princess Aisha?"

Barney's glasses had slipped down to the end of his

nose. He absently index-fingered them back onto the bridge of his nose, more or less.

"I know everything."

"And that," said Cody, "is why I'm here."

Barney snapped his fingers like someone really disappointed.

"Damn, and I thought you came all this way because you like the taste of my coffee."

Cody glanced into his cup and winced.

"Is that what you call it?" He finished the cup's contents with a slurp and set the cup down. He brought out his phone and dragged the pictures he'd loaded from Tiff Butler's phone in the restaurant; the photos of Sara Durrell's encounter with the two men at the Ms. Justice rally and the pics he'd taken of a dead guy's fingerprints and ear after the restaurant fracas. He handed the phone to Barney. "I'd like an ID on these two males and their present whereabouts, and an ID from those prints and ear shot. Can do?"

"On it," said Barney, turning to his PC. "Take a load off, dude. You look like you could use a breather. This shouldn't take long."

His fingers began blurring across the keyboard and utilizing the mouse. With initiating tasks begun, he handed the phone back to Cody. A peek over Barney's shoulder and Cody recognized US Government facial recognition software on one-half the screen, the government's NICS fingerprint data base coming up on the other half. Barney utilized all manner of uber tech he had no business having access to, having mastered it to an intuitive, Zen-like level of genius.

Cody found a chair and went about inserting into his phone the flash drive he'd retrieved from the hallway outside Sarah's apartment.

He used speed-read, quickly perusing the data and intel that had led Sara, without official sanction, to the Justice event where she was attacked. Her file was basically a well-organized dossier substantiating what she'd been able to convey to Cody during their communication in her hospital room: Thelma Justice and Princess Aisha were vaguely connected with the as yet unsubstantiated rumors of an ancient artifact of extreme significance with its modern implications.

"Whatever that young woman's got her hands on . . ." he muttered to no one but himself.

This situation had brought into play quite a collection of women, from a missing princess to a media mega star, from Tiff Butler who killed a man to save Cody's life to a crazy Russian wild child named Tanya. . . all of them overshadowed and outshone by the one woman who meant more to Cody than anyone or anything else.

He had to get Sara out of that damn hospital.

Barney turned from his computer.

"You want BG on the living or the dead first?"

"Let's give the living priority."

Barney brought up a pair of side-by-side passport photos on his PC screen. Arab males. Cody recognized one of them whose photo had been included in Sara's flash drive file; the one who'd sucker punched her at the rally.

He said, "Achmed al-Ahmad. Aisha's brother. That means the girl's family has her back in their custody. Present location?"

"Not yet. I need a little more time on that angle. Uh, who's the lady in the picture using the blade?"

"Let's just call her a friend."

Barney nodded approvingly.

"Whoever she is, she's handy with it. The guy she's carving up, that's Ali Yusef. Achmed's top enforcer."

"Duly noted. Which brings us to the dead."

"Ah, now it gets interesting. Your dead guy—at least he looked dead in the pictures you took of him—turned up only one good fingerprint photo and it came from the Swiss Ministry of Defense."

"The Swiss share a border with Italy. And?"

The dead hit man's passport photo lit up the PC screen.

Barney said, "Name's Bennicio Demaso. Served with distinction in the Swiss Armed Forces; distinction enough to rate recruitment by the Vatican's Swiss Guard."

"The Vatican?" Cody raised an eyebrow. "You're kidding."

"I don't kid," said Barney. "When last heard from, the late Bennicio had taken early retirement and was doing quite well in the freelance sector."

"Until tonight. So now the Vatican's elite security force drops into the mix. Okay, let's follow up that angle."

"I'll get on it," said Barney. "You think this Demaso could still be taking orders from the Vatican?"

"When he and that team came at me tonight, they were taking orders from somebody. The more I reflect on it, those guys that hit the restaurant didn't come to kill. They wanted to spirit away the woman I was with to learn what she knew. They'd tried for the princess at the Thelma Justice rally but lost her to Achmed and Yusef so they were grabbing at any straws they could find. They didn't expect me to be there."

"From what I heard on the police band, that's putting it mildly," said Barney, pouring himself another cup of coffee. He offered to refill Cody's cup. Cody declined. Barney noisily sipped his brew and added, "Something big is at stake here, buddy. Real big."

"It's either the princess or the relic she's supposedly in possession of," Cody agreed with a nod, "or both. Big enough to bring her brother Achmed all the way to DC hunting his kid sister and going up against a Vatican secret ops unit also hot on her trail."

"Christianity and a Muslim monarchy chasing after a young woman and her secret artifact," Barney summarized. "Gotcha. Anything else?"

"Yeah, now that you ask." Cody eyed the raucous club scene below. "You don't happen to run a grill in this joint?"

"Nope. Plenty to make your mouth water but no eats."

"Damn. I sure could use a burger. Okay, Barney. You got my number from the phone. Stay in touch."

CHAPTER EIGHTEEN

PINPRICKS of light shone through the cross-weave of burlap threads.

Aisha told herself that at least she could see light. The hood's coarse fibers itched irritably against the bruises she'd sustained during her abduction. There was no other word for it. The confusion of the attack at the Thelma Justice conference was a fresh storm roiling through her mind. Having witnessed the assault on the woman who'd accosted her and still reeling from the attack in the meeting room, she'd run for her life.

Who was the woman who approached her as she was leaving the scene of slaughter? She'd identified herself as working for the US government. But who was she? Aisha's mind was not clear enough to think about that now.

She ran, yes. But they cornered her within a few paces. They pounced upon her. They? Who were *they*? So many questions! The slaying of those Furies was proof enough that this was all about her, the Princess, and how they would stop at nothing.

She'd tried to fight them off like a spirit possessed, which in fact was exactly the case. Her mind, her spirit, her soul had been appreciating every breath of freedom since eluding her guard detail in England, especially since touching down in America—the Land of the Free —and being so graciously received under the auspices of Thelma Justice. Aisha had vowed to herself that she would fight to her death before ever submitting again to life in captivity.

And yet here she was, seated on a metal folding chair, its back pressing uncomfortably against her biceps, stretching her arms in numbing agony. Her wrists strained against the handcuffs that linked her wrists together.

With a crowd of onlookers everywhere about them, her abductors overpowered her in plain sight. Fast, well-executed teamwork, not thugs but a skilled paramilitary unit allowing no chance for onlookers to intercede. The security force had been drawn to the aftermath of violence in Meeting Room 12-B. Aisha had felt the prick of a needle and then lost consciousness.

She recovered consciousness feeling groggy, as if she'd awakened and was trying to recall final thoughts before falling asleep. She couldn't see much, wearing the burlap hood, but she could feel and hear. She felt closeness. She was in a small room. The air was warm. She detected her own scent and was glad she was wearing perfume. And close by . . . *someone breathing;* a shallow, normal, steady breathing, not excited or lascivious but constant. Nerve-wracking.

"Please," she said. "Remove this hood. And may I have a drink of water please?"

She was answered with a splash of water at the burlap that covered her head. She gasped. Droplets seeped through the burlap to trickle down her throat. She coughed, struggling to retain her regular breathing.

A man said in Arabic, "Is that enough water for you, Princess?"

She recognized that voice. It was her brother's right-hand man. His laugh was nasty, cruel. The laugh ended abruptly when a second man spoke, also in Arabic.

"Careful, Yusef," a stern familiar voice reprimanded. "Do not overstep your station."

Her older brother's voice always had the hollow, metallic sound of a speaker phone. Aisha recognized it instantly.

"Achmed, this is an outrage! Remove this hood at once."

From beneath the burlap hood, she could envision Achmed's lips curling into a mocking smile.

"The princess would speak as a queen. Mind your tongue, sister. The family is most displeased with you."

Aisha said, "Where are we?"

"That hardly matters. You won't be here long. I have been dispatched to return you home."

With one yank, Achmed removed the burlap hood from her head.

They were in a small, windowless room that could have been anywhere, Aisha's chair being the only furniture in the room. There was her brother with the second man, Yusef, whom she recognized. Yusef's left arm was heavily bandaged from where the American woman had carved him with her hair comb knife.

The difference in age and gender had erased any family similarity between Aisha and Achmed. Her brother was of average height, always well-dressed. Arrogant, aristocratic in demeanor and behavior.

She said, "Did our father sanction the slaughter of

those women, the Furies? Please do not say that is so. Those women only wished to help me. They did not deserve to die!"

"Banish such thoughts from your mind," said Achmed. "I do not deal in wholesale slaughter. Another party launched the attack on those who were hosting you. I was there with Yusef and his men. We made use of the confusion after that attack to take possession of you."

"Take possession?" Contempt dripped from the words. "Achmed, this is America, not Dubai. People do not *own* each other here."

"Those who did the killing," said Achmed. "We rescued you from them."

She struggled visibly against her bonds.

"Little difference," she sneered. "You shall pay, and greatly, for what you are doing. Here in America you are guilty of kidnapping and any manner of misdeeds. Release me. I demand it."

"Enough of this idle chatter." Achmed spoke to Yusef. "Prepare her for transport."

Alarm surged through her.

"No! I'm *not* going back."

"Silence!" said Achmed

Yusef said, "I could restrain her further."

"No. Once she is in the shipping crate, we will not hear from her until we reach our destination."

"Shipping crate?!"

Aisha trembled with indignation.

"You are reaping what you have sown," said Achmed. "Your insolence and misbehavior have brought disgrace upon our name."

She recalled her brother's enthusiasm when he'd participated in dispensing previous disciplinary measures against her. Achmed had wielded the rider's crop, removing its flat, energy-dispersing tip, against the soles of her feet, a place which would rarely show bruises. When used on horses, it was usually the spatula-like end which did the striking. Because all of the energy was spread out over a couple of square inches, the sting was negligible, a means of guiding a horse rather than torturing it into activity. When Achmed brought the narrow, flexible shaft of the crop across her feet in times past, all its force was concentrated into a tight area; torturous, never a mere one or two slaps. Always a dozen or more, after which Aisha would be expected to walk barefoot on raw, sometimes broken skin.

She said, "What can I do to win your mercy, my brother? To compel you to treat me like a human being? Like a sister?"

"Enough, I say," snapped Achmed. "If you persist, I will order Yusef to gag you. We are taking you home. It is useless to resist or object. I am but an instrument of Allah's will."

"Lie to yourself if you must," said Aisha. "You take pleasure in hurting women. You are not a healthy man, Achmed. I mourn for you. You cloak yourself in right-eousness but at your core you are a perverted deviant."

Achmed said to Yusef, "Remove her shoes."

Aisha gritted her teeth, continuing to struggle in vain against her restraints. Her chair flipped onto its back. She thought she was going to crack her skull on the bear floor but instead, Yusef caught the back of the chair, lowering her easily to the floor. Her ankles had been bound to the legs of the chair.

Yusef said, "Should I find something to use as a whip?"

"What good would it do?" said Achmed. "Our father has only commanded that she be located and returned home. Appropriate punishment will be determined. This will suffice . . . for now." He glared at Aisha. "Bear in mind that I can punish you at any time unless you behave. And consider yourself lucky, sister, that I am not as evil as you think me to be."

CHAPTER NINETEEN

Chief of Staff James Corbett studied President Harwood's agenda pad for the coming day. Corbett had thinning sandy hair, combed over. He was bespectacled with a studious demeanor.

At 0445 on this dark morning he was preparing for the coming twelve hours—at least!—that, like any West Wing day, would require him to function in nonstop adapt-and-improvise mode due to the very nature of his job. Like any day serving in this dynamic administration, his and the president's White House agenda looked good on paper but every day delivered its unexpected challenges, often minute by minute.

His phone sang its instant message note. Corbett turned it over for a glance at the screen.

The text read: "FACE TIME. FIFTEEN MINUTES? Sender: *Cory Jackson*".

Such a thinly veiled alias for one of the very few field agents the president stayed in personal touch with. There could be no mistaking it. And Cody would somehow have ID sufficient to gain entry. But just to make certain,

Corbett referred to his personal planner. He was right. The message came from the account Sara Durrell had set up for Jack Cody, verified by the White House phone system's electronic encryption programs.

Corbett touched the menu on his desk phone.

A crisp voice answered on the first ring.

"Southwest gate."

"This is Chief of Staff Corbett. I'm expecting a guest. Please provide him escort to the Mess. The name is Cory Jackson. "

The briefest instant while the soldier entered the name in his computer.

"Yes, sir. We'll be expecting him."

"Thank you."

Corbett ended the connection. Today's unexpected challenge, it seemed, was upon him. He had nothing against Cody personally.

As "the president's man," Cody, a dark ops ace without peer, had performed a number of heroic missions in recent months. But from the beginning Corbett had been leery about the entire Cody situation. Cody was a field agent with an incredible success record dating to the previous administration. But then had come the tragedy of losing his family to terrorists, of going rogue, annihilating those terrorists and then, well, his mental breakdown and withdrawal. Understandable. Cody eventually recovered and returned to work.

With his one damn stipulation.

Cody would only take on assignments that were suicide missions with little or no chance of survival. A stipulation only a top hand could make and his was deemed acceptable in order to get a man of his abilities back into the field on key missions. Indeed, although Greb Vetrov was still on the loose, the nukes the general had tried to sell North Korea were back in official hands. The Russian government had recovered all twelve warheads, although a couple were damaged. The detonation mechanisms, fortunately. The casings were intact. Moscow was happy with all of the assistance rendered by the US in learning of the deal and canceling it out. US-Russian relations were enhanced thanks to the efforts of this one incredible warrior.

Cody had succeeded on every one of those so called "suicide missions" they'd sent him on. But that could not go on forever. Those in the know had already tagged him with the nickname Suicide. The Harwood administration was essentially enabling a man in his effort to kill himself. It was like what they called "suicide by cop." How could they say a man was back to being well-adjusted when he was using these missions in an attempt to end his life? Corbett had voiced these concerns in cabinet meetings. His sentiments were shared somewhat by the president and others but the gravity and urgency driving such missions had taken precedence. That too was understandable.

Corbett rubbed his eyes. It was a quarter hour walk to the staff dining area in the West Basement of the White House. He'd best get under way. Time for face time with Jack Cody, a.k.a. Cory Jackson.

"Nikki."

His assistant, a young black woman, poked her head around the corner of his office door, smiling.

"Yes, sir?"

"Something's come up. Could you do a quick once over of the schedule for me?"

Nikki nodded. She possessed a perky nature even at this hour.

"It's on the server?"

"It is. Thanks. If anyone asks, I'll be in the Mess."

Nikki looked at her watch.

"Uh, sir. You'll be there just in time for fresh bagels."

Corbett smiled.

"Blueberry?"

"Thanks."

His walk to the West Basement, through a busy maze of offices and corridors that buzzed with activity 24 hours a day, allowed him the opportunity to review and consider the matter at hand.

Cody's CIA control officer, Sara Durrell, had attended a Thelma Justice event concerning

an international missing person's case. Durrell had been assaulted after an attack that left several Justice security personnel dead and was presently at Bethesda Naval hospital under guard. A personal relationship existed between Cody and Durrell of a romantic nature. Cody had apparently again gone rogue but not before President Harwood assured him that he would keep a personal eye on the situation, thus dropping the ball squarely into Corbett's lap.

When he reached the Mess, he immediately spotted Cody with his Marine escort, as was common for guests of White House staff when invited into the Mess.

Though nominally called a Mess, the large room was warm and adorned with wooden paneling, pillars interspersed among space for a seating capacity of at least fifty. There were only a few people at the tables in the eating area this early. One wall of the room was dominated by the painting of a three-masted Naval vessel from the early 1800's. Cream carpet and track lighting in white ceilings brightened the dark wooden walls and pillars, and an even row of historic Naval vessel portraits stretched at eye level. Off to one side, there was a line of staffers waiting at the Mess' takeout window.

Corbett said, "Good morning, Mr. Jackson."

He and Cody shook hands.

The marine remained stoic at parade rest.

"Sir. "

"I've got him from here," Corbett assured the Marine.

The escort about-faced and left.

Corbett led them to a wall table without either speaking. An attendant, dressed in white shirt, black vest and dark slacks, placed saucers and coffee cups before Corbett and Cody.

"Regular or unleaded? "

"Regular, " said Cody.

"High octane if you please," Corbett requested.

The attendant poured from the same silver carafe for them both.

"Something to eat, gentlemen?"

Cody asked, "Is it too early to order up a burger, fries and a Coke?"

"Never too early for meat and potatoes," he grinned. "And you, sir?"

"Shit on a shingle, " said Corbett, "and a blueberry bagel with cream cheese to go."

Another grin from the attendant at Corbett's order for Creamed Chipped Beef on Bread, a military staple since 1910—and its loving nickname.

"Very well, sir."

Corbett was an Army man. He caught the attendant's grin as the young man turned to leave with their order.

"What can I say?" Corbett chuckled in mild apology for the off color-language. "Old habits die hard."

When their server had withdrawn beyond earshot, Cody slid Sara Durrell's flash drive file across the table to Corbett. The Chief of Staff regarded him with an arched eyebrow before inserting the flash drive in his phone. He then proceeded to spend some time considering what he read with a furrowed brow.

During these passing minutes, Cody said nothing. A brief respite in physical movement and exertion in the grueling nonstop pace of this night, the interlude was rejuvenating more than relaxing. Cody's mind was functioning sharply enough but a man's system could only absorb so much without needing sustenance between rounds.

Breakfast came as Corbett completed his perusal of the file. He pocketed his phone, making no attempt to return the flash drive. The White House Mess was a place of discreetly discussed high security matters. The attendant, true to his professionalism as a Navy Ensign, studiously ignored anything but serving their dishes and leaving them to their discussion.

Corbett's brow hadn't lost its furrows. He ate his first forkful of beef, roux and bread.

"Your friend Durrell compiled quite a file on the princess, including her reasons and intent in pursuing the matter at the Justice event. But I'm not sure it doesn't corroborate Jared Parnell's charges against her more than it refutes them."

Cody said nothing until after thoroughly chewing and swallowing his first mouthful of hamburger followed by fries and a gulp of Coca-Cola.

Then he said, "Ah, perfect. Worth the wait." Then he returned his attention to the man across from him. "Mr. Corbett, we'll save time if I know how tuned in you are on what's been going down tonight."

"About what you'd expect," said Corbett. "This is the White House. We know everything. At least we know most of what has occurred. You know how the president feels about you. He's had me monitoring reports of Parnell's people. That was a pretty slick job, dodging their surveillance at the Durrell apartment. We lost you after hot contact at that restaurant."

Cody said, "Parnell. He's got me and Sara wired, or thinks he has. Sir, I don't believe he's at all concerned about her, quote, abuse of government resources or our personal affairs after hours. Parnell has his own reasons and I am going to find out what they are."

"Princess Aisha's family wants her back, and they aren't afraid to crack some eggs to bring her home. Were they the ones behind the slaughter of those Justice security personnel?"

"I don't figure it that way," said Cody between bites. "Achmed wants to get her home to make their papa happy but not enough to raise an international incident like that. A better bet would be the unit that brought on the restaurant fire fight."

"The police are calling it a failed robbery."

Cody shook his head.

"That's what the police would say. This is way over their head. Trace someone named Bennicio Demaso, late of the Vatican's Swiss Guard."

Corbett stopped eating, eyeing Cody with a skeptical eye.

"The Vatican? How the hell—?"

"Trust me."

"And who do you trust?" Corbett asked.

"I trust you, sir because you speak for the president. I can't much afford to trust anyone else at this point. And with this ball in play, sir, I can't much afford to cool my heels for long in one place." He finished the burger and fries. The Coke brought a muted, contented burp. "Give my regards to POTUS. I've got to be pushing on."

"Police reports mention a gunman fled with a woman."

"No comment."

"I don't think that will do."

"It'll have to for now."

Corbett's eyes narrowed.

"You're operating with a mighty free hand, mister."

Cody ignored the remark.

He said, "Secure Sara's release from the hospital if you or the president can. She's earned her position through nothing but honesty and hard work. Her reputation at the agency is impeccable. I'm the closest thing to a stain on her record until Parnell came along."

Corbett nodded. "I'll see what I can do, Jack."

Cody gave a grunt of affirmation.

Corbett said, "Sure you're not trying to convince yourself?"

Cody shook his head.

"I'm not. I trust Sara. I sure as hell don't trust Parnell."

Corbett chose not to mention that, much as he respected Cody, he in some ways shared Parnell's apparent opinion that the Suicide Cody setup was less than ideal.

Corbett said, "Your next move?"

"Sara was interested in an artifact that Aisha was in possession of, which seems worth enough to draw in the attention of Justice, of the Vatican, and of her own family. And if it draws in a multi-billionaire and one of the world's most influential nation states, I'm going to want to see what this artifact is about.

"If Achmed has her, he's going to be in a hurry to get both Aisha and the artifact home if they're together. If they're not together, I might find her fast enough to figure what is going on with the artifact, and why it's so important."

Corbett took a sip of his coffee.

"All of this will get sidetracked, you understand, if new intel on Vetrov should develop. You planted his shipment of his warheads at the bottom of a crevice in the Urals, but the man's nothing if not resourceful."

"Right now, he's tapped for customers. I'm sure North Korea won't be happy over being stiffed. He's already on INTERPOL's shit list, and he's being hunted by the Russian authorities. Parnell should be monitoring their chatter for cues on Vetrov, but of course he seems more interested in me and Sara."

"I'll try to cool Parnell's heels," said Corbett.

Cody rose from their table. They shook hands. Then Cody turned away.

Corbett's lips tightened into a thin line. Yes, he had his reservations about the Cody issue. But he would never bear anything but the highest regard and respect for the man.

"Good luck, soldier," he whispered silently to Cody's back.

Then the magnificent guy and his Marine escort were lost from view across the busy mess area. Corbett picked up the little white bag containing Nikki's bagel. He hurried with it and his troubled mind back through the West Wing.

The "Cody issue" had just gotten worse.

The president would *not* be pleased.

CHAPTER TWENTY

PRESIDENT HARWOOD HAD ONLY BEEN AWAKE a few hours but already felt like he could use a power nap.

He may have appeared a decade or more younger than his mid-sixties, but inside Harwood felt the grinding drag of the presidency. Men who came to his job with dark, thick hair left office with a few more inches of forehead with salt and pepper replacing the vibrancy of their youth. Harwood's facial features already hinted outwardly at the effects of a job high in 24-7 stress, his cheekbones having morphed from full and strong to looking like curtain rods for sallow, sunken jowls. The small club of living presidents consisted of men bonded by this one-of-a-kind job and its inherent, nonstop stress.

There was a knock at his door.

Harwood rose to respond. Wanting to escape the soul-crushing gravity of his desk in the Oval Office, he'd found privacy in the small Lincoln Sitting Room.

"Come in, Jim."

James Corbett entered.

"Good morning, Mr. President."

"That," growled the president, "is yet to be determined." He indicated the manila folder Corbett held. "I don't expect you sought me out on a minor matter."

Corbett handed him the folder.

"Not hardly. You requested a briefing on my visit with Cody. I stopped by my office only to drop off a bagel for my secretary and to have this hard copy made for you."

Harwood went to the small desk and scanned through the folder's contents while Corbett went to the coffee maker and poured himself a mug. The president frowned. He looked up from the folder.

"Jack Cody gave this to you?"

"Yes, sir. It's a dossier compiled by Sara Durrell regarding that Middle Eastern princess who went missing after those murders at the Ms. Justice event." Corbett downed a gulp of black coffee, wanting all of the caffeine he could get. "D.C. is jumping right now. Several local and federal agencies have an APB out on her."

Harwood considered an item in the dossier that caught his eye.

"Says here Achmed al-Ahmad may have ties to a criminal smuggling enterprise."

"Or they approached him because of his importance."

"One billionaire superstar with a paramilitary female security force and a billionaire's son likely linked to Middle Eastern cartels?" Harwood sighed. He closed the folder. "How's Jack doing?"

"In a word, he's gone vigilante. Jared Parnell's got him seeing red. Frankly, sir, I'd bet on this situation getting one hell of a lot hotter before it's over." Corbett cleared his throat. "And, uh, Cody could use our help beyond us simply monitoring him."

The president regarded his chief of staff with a trace of amusement.

"I wouldn't have expected you to say that, Jim. You haven't been exactly enthusiastic about the whole Cody thing from the beginning."

Corbett gave a small shrug.

"I know, after the reservations I've put forth. But something is going on with this business that we need to settle before it spins completely out of control and more people die. There's no doubting Cody's effectiveness and his primary resource right now is currently under lock and key."

Harwood pinched his wrinkling brow.

"Sara Durrell."

Corbett nodded, sipping more coffee from his mug.

"I'm wondering if we could get her released under her own recognizance. Should be a safe bet. She took one hell of a shellacking."

"Why the hell should she be restricted in the first place," said the president, "simply for looking into the Princess Aisha business?" He emitted a grunt of displeasure. "It's as if someone inside the CIA doesn't want the matter looked into. Could we be dealing with a mole?"

Corbett gave that a moment's consideration, then responded with the mildest of shrugs.

"Anything is possible. But to me this smells more like internal agency politicking. I'll make a point of pinning down Parnell to see what he has to say without alerting anyone who is abusing their powers that we're on to them."

Harwood said, "I saw something on the local news feed a short while ago about some restaurant shooting.

Three dead. Cody's name didn't come up but it certainly looks like his handiwork." The president chuckled in spite of himself. "The restaurant in question is only blocks from Sara Durrell's apartment. When something like that goes down and Cody's in town, I can't help jumping to conclusions."

"You're right jumping to that conclusion," said Corbett. "Three gunmen closed in on Cody and a woman in that restaurant. The gunmen went down."

"Woman?"

"She left with Cody. I asked him about her. He dodged the question. Wish I could have gotten this to you before the Presidential Daily Briefing but I needed to confirm and that came in too late."

"So we have no clue who the woman was or the three dead men? Cody had to give you something."

"Not much, I'm afraid. Just enough to let me know he is getting somewhere. We've got the name of a professional merc who used to be in the Vatican's Swiss guard. He was one of the dead guys in the restaurant."

Harwood's frown grew deeper, darker.

"The Vatican? Jim, this is no time for levity."

"Wish I was kidding," said Corbett, "but you and I both know you can't make this shit up and neither can Cody. We're tracing the name he gave us but so far nothing but firewalls."

"Stay on it. This has got to be tied in somehow with the death of those Thelma Justice security women. Like Cody being in town and the shooting starts, I don't believe in coincidence."

Corbett took a sip from his mug. The conversation had gone on long enough that the coffee was no longer scalding hot.

"There is the possibility of a connection. Given the

highly selective recruitment process the Order of World Harmony uses for the Furies, their security apparatus is made up of only the best and brightest from military, police and federal agencies around the world. The women in that organization are armed and they're skilled. Top shelf all the way."

"They weren't good enough to protect the princess."

"We're uncertain," said Corbett, "if that was due to a lack of a sufficient security personnel or if security was adequate but simply overpowered by a superior force. Thelma Justice has been in seclusion but spokeswomen for The Order of World Harmony have been pressuring for action, calling the death of those Furies a terrorist act."

"Which puts this administration front and center in every way there is," said Harwood. "Mass killings and kidnapping in the heart of our nation's capital are not what we promised the American people. We've got to turn this around. Thelma Justice has every right to demand answers and action. The woman contributed even more than her share to help get me elected."

"She's one of the good guys," Corbett agreed with a nod. "Fact is, my wife reads her books and watches her every day on TV. Has Thelma made direct contact with you?"

Harwood sighed, deeper than before.

"Not yet. The hard cold truth is we can't be certain that she isn't a rogue entity."

Ms. Justice's enormous wealth was a web that crisscrossed the globe, no more so than in Washington. Her media influence had translated into even more financial wealth and international influence. Her appearance in Washington was one of the few times she'd made an in-person appearance on U.S. soil. Usually, the guru and spiritual leader of The Order of World Harmony found solace in the Italian Alps in a chalet/fortress high atop a formidable mountain range. Even so, when Thelma Justice got it in her mind to do something, her whispers swiftly raced across the Atlantic and found their way to the right ears.

Corbett drained his coffee mug and set it aside. With a sigh of his own, he eyed the first gray hint of dawn seeping into the Lincoln Sitting Room.

"This mess spilling out of bounds fast as it has from so many angles at once, it's going to be one hell of a day."

"Amen to that," said Harwood. "Jack Cody sure as hell picked the right time to come home."

CHAPTER TWENTY-ONE

THELMA JUSTICE DREW her lips from those of Greb Vetrov, the heat and wet passion of their tongue kiss sticky and slow to release, even seeming to resist their pull from each other.

Her chin felt raw from his rough stubble grating during their wild, insane lovemaking. She ran her fingers over the short buzzed scrub of her man's skull, tracing the scar tissue he'd accrued over his years in both military and civilian life.

Vetrov grinned, his steely blue eyes meeting her deep brown pools with a spent, icy abandon. The impressions of her passionately nibbling teeth remained across his lower lip. The long scratches from her nails, inflicted during the heights of her multiple orgasms, crisscrossed and burned his back.

They were breathless. Thelma's shoulders glistened like hard candy, freckles dotting her neck and shoulders where his calloused hands had commanded her flesh.

Vetrov tongued her ear.

"If this is how you reward failure . . ."

Thelma was still catching her breath.

"You mean those missiles you lost in Russia? We still have the Koreans' down payment, and we don't have to worry about that inbred gook royalty having them. We are too close to initiating *our* action. Aren't we, darling?"

Vetrov chuckled.

"Yes indeed. A world of perfect feminine beauty, isn't that your vision? A world where women rule and men are little more than domesticated seed bearers. No war, no famine . . . But first the rubble of male domination must be scorched from the face of the earth. This is worth a global nuclear catastrophe which we, you and I, shall orchestrate. Is that not a fair summation?" He shook his head with a twist of his lips that could have been a smile. He added, "Why do you want such a boring world? This intrigues me, you little slut."

Thelma smirked. She leaned in to kiss him hungrily, again biting his tongue, then his lip before she pulled away.

She said, "You are irredeemable."

"Am I?"

"A man like you is a necessary evil. Ms. Justice might as well make the best of it and take her pleasure as the day of judgment approaches."

Vetrov laughed lustily, loudly slapping her ass with an open palm.

"My little slut has ambition. I think you'll do a fine job ruling the world. You do of course realize there was no shortage of wars and civil strife during the time when goddesses ruled."

Thelma slid off of him and off of the bed. She picked up her robe and drew it carelessly about her shoulders. She sashayed into the bathroom.

Vetrov rolled onto his side, resting his jaw on his hand.

"Without me, the patriarchy would triumph over you by simply outgunning you in every way."

"And with you," Thelma said, "I have all the elements of toxic masculinity . . . that I clearly despise."

"Despise . . . and need." His laugh ground at her nerves. "That's the problem with a radical such as you, Thelma. You seek all or nothing."

She cleansed herself.

"How would you know?"

"Because I want the same."

Thelma paused in her ablutions. She peered around the door jamb from the washroom and regarded the Russian, stretched out upon his back. Fingers clasped behind his head. A smug grin on his craggy features.

My little slut.

Everyone else in the world treated her like the goddess she was. Greb knew her deepest lusts and hungers. Those things in the bedroom kept her coming back for more. Early in life—while still in her teens, in fact—she had begun with a conscious, determined obsession, to reconstruct herself; to transform, to polish and hone, ingraining in herself those three unspoken, universal aspects of "the complete woman."

Lady in the parlor.

Chef in the kitchen.

Slut in the bedroom.

She and Vetrov had been lovers now for more than a year. Only her disciplined faculty for compartmentalization had kept their top secret affair from being more complicated than it already was. Sexually, she had always preferred women—girls—until this man. It had never concerned her that her time with him between the sheets

—the raging, overheated sex; the arousal and total satisfaction—meant anything more than an ephemeral, pleasurable episode. A woman satisfied her needs. Afterward, she should expect and was entitled to her privacy.

The Order of World Harmony would one day soon envelope the world; a new world order rising from nuclear ash. Women would rule the world. And this man, embodying all she despised and lusted after, was the means by which she would make that happen.

She said, "You pretend to seek power through me. To conquer. But in truth you want only to destroy. You want the world to burn."

Vetrov chuckled.

"Only that which I despise, like this town of corruption and lies."

"And what else do you despise?"

He gazed at the ceiling as if occupied with its bubbly popcorn pattern.

"Enough of the same things that you hate that we get along."

Thelma stepped back and returned to her personal ministrations.

"So you say."

"So I *know*." Vetrov's tone and expression grew dark. "The world is engulfed in a confederacy of incompetence, falsehood and greed. You and I, we both hate those who wield the reins, though for admittedly different reasons. Still, together we shall scourge administrations and burn their ivory towers to blackened bones."

Scratch even the hardest, obstinate Russian soldier, thought Thelma, *and you'll find a failed poet.*

For Soviet Cold War veterans like Greb, the 21st century had become a dark age. Despite the internet and countless means to access knowledge, the march of

American-style capitalism continued to sweep the world, taking his beloved Mother Russia and irredeemably soiling her. Thelma had come to understand the depths to which Vetrov despised "The American Way." He considered it a festering plague. America didn't need its armies to crush nations. It conquered with greasy pink slime crafted into hamburgers and saturated fats that stole the strength and vigor of the Russian man. Corn syrup and artificial sweeteners took the brain and addicted it to one or the other, sapping the intellect. Electronic devices and mindless applications had replaced innovation and ambition. America might not have built the electronic platforms but it was creating an ever-constricting snare of inanity known as the World Wide Web, seizing the world's best and brightest minds and then poisoning and drowning them in fluff and frivolity. Vetrov wanted that world forever cleansed of such pollutants.

True, he stank of cigarettes and vodka. He was gruff and grizzled, and he worshipped the power of the gun and the bomb. But he radiated a magnetism—sensual *and* intellectual—that Thelma found herself unable to ignore or resist. They were equals in audacity and ambition. He matched her seething anger most passionately during their savage coupling.

He'd told her about Jack Cody, who'd interfered with his operation in Russia before eluding him in a suicidal leap off of a crashing train, the growled words heavy with hatred, anger and frustration at that outcome matched her frustration over having "lost" Princess Aisha.

Thelma dressed quickly, and regarded herself in the mirror. No makeup, and she wrapped her signature curls beneath a headwrap. Sure, she was tall and imposing. But the way she looked now, few people would recognize her as the important television star that she was. Makeup artists cast her in an increasingly different light at her request so that she could disappear in a crowd. Rather than the top fashion name suits she wore, the charcoal off-the-rack suit she chose helped her blend in. The wrap shaved inches off of her height. She would be a stranger to anyone.

When she rejoined him, Vetrov remained unashamedly naked. He was reaching into the slim travel bag he'd arrived with.

"By the way," he said, "I've been thinking about your missing princess."

She prepared them each a shot of vodka.

"You have a sudden interest in my work?"

"I always do. But a kidnapped princess seems is something I could certainly sink my teeth into."

"I'm not here to supply you with snacks," Thelma growled."It's bad enough that I'm away from my compound. Being seen with you could cause too many problems."

They clinked glasses. Vetrov smirked.

"You worry too much about your public image," said Vetrov, "and my sloppiness. No one tracks Greb Vetrov!"

He referred to the screen of his phone.

"You have your resources, and I have mine."

He hefted the phone, if it could be called that. Vetrov's "telephone" was the size of a brick, wrapped in black rubber armor. The screen, however, was crisp and impressive.

Thelma said, "That looks like some primitive piece of equipment that fell off a truck in Siberia."

"It was manufactured in Sibera," replied Vetrov, "and it is indeed powered by a server from there. But it is made of the finest pirated soft and hardware that we could find."

"Then show me something more impressive."

He idly finger-scrolled his links on the screen.

"Very well. Perhaps we should take a dive into—"

His words trailed off. His expression grew intense. He stared at the screen, eyes narrowed and an almost visible anger coursing through him.

"What is it, Greb?"

"That . . . son of a bitch."

"Who?"

"This man."

He held the phone apparatus so she could see the screen: a big man, dark hair, with an ageless appearance —anywhere between thirty to fifty—with sharp, piercing eyes. Walking down a hallway. A security camera picture.

"Who is it?"

"That, my love, is Mr. Jack Cody, my would-be nemesis. He is the one who took down my shipment of warheads. The last time I saw him, he was throwing himself off a speeding train. I sat in a gunship's gunner seat, sweeping a mile of Ural mountain train tracks, looking for him or his corpse."

"Where is this photo from?"

"He's walking down a hallway in the White House. My assets in America have been instructed to channel to me any sighting. Cody, you see, is a most durable chap and I kept having this feeling I hadn't seen the last of him. White House facial recognition software tagged him and so this photo was sent did to me."

"I'm impressed," said Thelma. "Hacking the White House security camera system? Yes, very impressive."

Vetrov relaxed and said, "We continue to penetrate each other's mystery, no?"

"Among other things," she responded dryly.

"Being one of the richest men in the world does have its benefits," he said "Everyone and everything is for sale if you can meet the price . . . except for men like this, damn them. And to speak the truth, I never encountered a man like Jack Cody. I've researched him thoroughly."

"What a coincidence," said Thelma.

She told him about Tiff Butler's encounter with Cody in Sara Durrell's apartment. She told him about the restaurant shootout and subsequently losing track of Cody. Vetrov listened carefully, his eyes remained glued to Cody's image on the phone screen.

"Let us both initiate deep dive research to see if there are threads that could connect us."

"We found each other through our mutual ambitions," Thelma said. "And they found each of us through whatever drive makes them stick their noses in the affairs of gods."

"Gods, darling?"

Thelma glared at him.

"*We* are the center of the universe. We have the power right now to shake the entire world. These annoying worms must receive our fullest and immediate attention."

Vetrov grinned lasciviously.

"That's the woman I lust for. I should grab you right now and—"

"This room would burn," she snickered. "Important matters need attending to. Get up, you lazy dog. There's work to be done."

CHAPTER TWENTY-TWO

BARNEY LUND SAID, "You've got a tiger by the tail, buddy, and that sucker's gaining and ready to jump and swallow you alive."

"It's why I keep moving," said Cody. "Giving them a moving target is my defense strategy at this point."

"Good enough for now, I suppose," growled Barney, "but they've got you outnumbered, man. Best brotherly advice I can offer you would be to get your ass the hell out of DC and lie low for, oh, maybe a hundred years or so."

"I've been outnumbered before," said Cody. "So far we've got Parnell and that crew in the restaurant. Any other hit teams I should watch out for?"

Barney had picked up on the first ring with none of their standard opening back-and-forth banter. The call, routed through any number of satellite encoded relays, was crystal clear and hopefully untapped. An undercurrent edge of concern made Barney's voice tight.

He said, "Buddy, I had to do some real—I mean *real*

—deep diving to dredge up what intel I've come up with so far. You want the process or just the bottom line?"

"Make a guess."

"Right. Ever hear of the Congregation of the Doctrine of the Faith?"

"Aw, hell."

"Uh huh. Vatican dark ops. Rooted in ancient church history. An autonomous branch of the Dominicans founded centuries ago to oppose heresy; still operational, covertly of course. Basically the enforcement arm of the Catholic Church. Hit men for God. The Church vehemently denies their existence. The late Mr. Demaso was a field agent and unit commander. Given the context, I'd say this is tied in with your elusive princess. This ancient relic everyone talks about. Whispers about. That's right up those boys' alley."

"Speaking of the princess," said Cody, "what have you got there?"

"This mess you've gotten yourself into has too damn many angles," groused Barney. "Yeah, that was next on my get-to list. I trolled through Big Brother's tracking of Achmedal-Ahmad's credit cards, et cetera since they got the States this time. Layers of aliases and firewalls there too. But there's two dots our stellar government agencies have not yet managed to connect."

"But you have?"

Barney acknowledged this with an immodest, "Am I the man or what? Achmed's associate, Ali Yusef, carelessly acquired a vehicle from a rental agency using his own credit card. The rental agency just happens to be situated a few blocks from a transport business warehouse that's secretly owned by Aisha's family under one of their false fronts."

Cody extrapolated, "Achmed used the company's resources to track Aisha."

"It's near the Annapolis shipyards," said Barney. "If they are utilizing the warehouse, the plan could be to get her out of the country by sea."

"And no government agency has followed through on that lead?"

"They haven't put the jigsaw puzzle together as I have," said Barney, "because they don't know the al-Ahmad family secretly owns that warehouse."

He gave Cody the warehouse address.

"That's a strong enough lead to investigate," said Cody. "Thanks, Barney. I'll—"

Barney said, "Uh, one last thing before you go."

"What's that?"

"Greb Vetrov. He's in DC."

"And how sure are we of this?"

"Do you forget to whom you are speaking?"

"Sorry, Barn."

"I'm as sure as your gang at Langley because that's where I filched the info from. Mind you, they haven't bagged him yet but their intel is solid and is backed by the Russians who want to get their hands on Vetrov too. Maybe more so because he's their bad apple. So it took a while and came together piece by piece but I think we can bank it as solid."

"That's how far out in the cold I am," said Cody. "Something of that magnitude should have been related to me."

"No shit," agreed Barney. "After the way you tossed his salad over in the Urals, he could be here to personally take you out."

"A possibility," Cody agreed, "but Vetrov hasn't yet made a move that didn't have a monetary incentive. He has no love for me and he may be underground enjoying some R&R and that's why they can't locate him. But he's come here because there's a buyer here who wants to take some nukes off his hands. We can't let that happen."

"It would be nice if that damn Parnell was out of the picture," said Barney. "If Vetrov is such a threat, Parnell ought to dispense with agency politics and get you on it."

"There are a lot of things here that don't fit together the way they should," said Cody. "You got anything else for me, Barn?"

"I'd say you've got enough on your plate now," snorted Barney, "to last you until next Christmas. Maybe the Christmas after that. Watch your ass, Cody. I've only got one best friend. By the way, did you find that hamburger you were looking for?"

"I did and you won't believe where."

When Cody told him, Barney laughed out loud.

"Cody my man, you are one ballsy, crazy dude!"

"Doing my best," Cody assured him. "Thanks, Barney. Stay out of trouble and keep your head down. Things are about to heat up big time. It's a new day and that White House burger has me feeling like a new man. It's time to kick ass."

CHAPTER TWENTY-THREE

JARED PARNELL TOOK a hit off of his vape, trying to calm his bristling nerves. He sat waiting before the desk of Chief of Staff James Corbett's secretary.

Nikki didn't turn her head as she finished off her bagel spread with blueberry-flavored cream cheese, though she did demonstrate enough side-eye to remind Parnell of her dislike of his electronic cigarette. He pursed his lips and blew a stream of smoke that fogged the air between them.

The door of the inner office opened. It was Jim Corbett.

Parnell rose to his feet.

"You wanted to see me?"

He deliberately left off the *sir* customarily afforded Corbett's position.

"I called for you," Corbett acknowledged, "not for enough smoke screen to get troops across a no-man's land." He nodded at the vape pen. "Turn that shit off and into my office."

Parnell killed the e-cigarette. He followed Corbett

into the inner office, avoiding eye contact with the secretary who finished her bagel and returned to work on her computer. Corbett planted himself behind his desk. He did not invite Parnell to take one of the chairs that faced his desk. He spoke up sharply when Corbett started to sit down.

"What the hell do you think that you're doing?"

"I'm sitting down."

"No, you're not. You're not going to be here long enough."

"Then why am I here?"

Corbett locked eyes with him.

"You do know who Sara Durrell and Jack Cody are?"

Parnell bit his tongue, measuring his response. Play it cool, he told himself. He replied with a simple fact stated with a straight face.

"Durrell is Cody's control officer. Cody is a field operative the president occasionally selects for missions deemed too difficult for conventional operations."

Corbett nodded.

"Very good. So you can therefore understand that the president, who is personally fond of both of them, is concerned over Durrell's treatment and that of Cody. It's time for you to face up to this concern and explain yourself, Jared."

The use of his first name made the sharp words personal.

Parnell said in a milder voice than before, "I'm more than happy to offer any input that will clarify the situation, sir. I've achieved my present position in the CIA through years of—"

"Yes, yes. We know all of that. I've reviewed your file. The president and I want to know about this mad-on you have for Cody and Durrell. There is a renegade

Russian general on the loose, selling nukes on the open market for crying out loud. *He* is the driving focus of these two good, loyal people you would malign and it should be *your* focus, not banal personality issues."

Parnell said, "Sir, we're developing intel that Vetrov is in DC. I'm confident we'll track him down here and eliminate him as a threat, either apprehend him or apply extreme prejudice. We don't need a loose cannon cowboy like Jack Cody for that. We're using high tech and precision tactics. I want to clean out the dinosaurs, sir. My objective is to bring my department into the 21st century."

"Mister," said Corbett, "that's a slap in the face to your superiors and the two people we're talking about. That dinosaur Cody just saved millions of lives with his mission to stop Vetrov's deal with the North Koreans."

Parnell's response was canned and fast.

"Yes, sir. But that was luck. We can't always be lucky. We *can*, on the other hand, depend on technology and modern methods. Cody has already had one mental breakdown after what happened to his wife and children. With these missions he's being sent on, what if he has a relapse? It could happen. Look at the way he's gone rogue after learning of the mess Durrell has made for herself."

"Let's talk about that," said Corbett. "You keep talking about some flagrant misuse of power but I haven't seen any formal charges filed. What abuse of power, exactly?"

"First off as you well know, sir, the CIA is not mandated to utilize its resources on American soil."

"You're talking to the Chief of Staff, son. You want me to pretend there's not an unfortunate history of the CIA meddling in domestic affairs? It's not something I necessarily approve of but . . . hell, sometimes we need to think outside of the box when this country's best interests are at stake."

"Durrell was engaged in investigating Thelma Justice, a private citizen, without authorization or just cause."

"What about 'where there's smoke, there's fire'?" said Corbett. "That night Princess Aisha disappeared. Members of the Justice security force were assassinated during a kidnap attempt. Looks to me like Durrell was on to something."

"And there's this," pressed Parnell. "That all-woman security force of the Justice organization, The Furies of Harmony, has unknowingly taken in their employ several of our agents working undercover. As such we have eyes for example in one of Moscow's largest commerce buildings, the Beletoz Tower. A dinosaur like Cody ignores a place where Greb Vetrov has been known to hang his hat. The Order of World Harmony has offices there. We've been angling for some time to get a CIA analyst embedded there. It seemed like an impossible task and had taken awhile to set up but is close to being accomplished with, I might add, considerable finesse."

Corbett leaned back and steepled his fingers.

"As opposed to?"

"As opposed to Cody swings from grappling hooks through windows in black spandex and a shoulder holster. For chrissake, sir, the CIA doesn't kick down doors. That's what the meatheads in the military are for. If we're going to keep pace with the Russian Federation and the People's Republic of China, we have to stop pretending that *In Like Flint* is a relevant depiction of modern espionage."

Corbett rolled his eyes.

"I'm surprised you even know that movie."

"James Coburn. Great garbage fun on cable," said Parnell. "But in terms of up to date—"

"How would a SEAL Team have handled the thing in the Ural more efficiently?" Corbett asked. "It would have taken longer to assemble and stage a team insertion. Cody worked his assets, not only locating where Vetrov had stashed the cargo but he went on to destroy those nukes on their way to the coast."

Parnell closed his eyes.

"Sir, the issue with Durrell is that she saw fit to interfere with—"

"The al-Ahmad royal family's domestic stability, which is in fact a matter of our concern in a geopolitical context. Should the CIA disregard murder and the kidnapping of the princess?"

"The family, represented by her brother, has located her before," said Parnell, "without interference from us. Because of those geopolitical dynamics, I feel we must tread lightly so as not to offend him and alienate the al-Ahmad family who are trusted allies in a hostile region. That's the whole thing. Cody tromps about like a rampaging triceratops, not showing the slightest subtlety nor concern for who or what he destroys in the process."

Corbett sighed but his hard demeanor remained as if carved in stone.

He said, "Sara Durrell only had the best interests of Princess Aisha in mind, of that I'm certain. From what I've read about Achmed al-Ahmad, her safety is hardly guaranteed while in her family's custody. But let's keep this about Sara. The president does not like her being held as a jailed criminal."

Parnell's lips drew into a taut line.

"Sir, are you instructing me to coddle these

dinosaurs? To leave us vulnerable to clever bastards like Vetrov?"

Corbett met that remark with a new edge in his steely gaze.

"Maybe we should check on *your* abuse of power. Clean up your game, Jared, or I'll step in and clean it up for you. That is all. You may leave."

"But sir, about Cody—"

"I said that's all, Parnell. Dismissed."

CHAPTER TWENTY-FOUR

THE SUN WAS a brilliant orange ball inching its way up from the horizon.

Cody's dive sliced smoothly into the blue-black waters of Chesapeake Bay, just a little south of Annapolis; a half-mile from the warehouse and private dock of the secretly owned al-Ahmad import/export company. Under water in a dry suit, he was protected from the chill of the Atlantic that here flowed northward around the Delmarva peninsula, around the so-called "belly and legs" area of its shrimp profile.

He hadn't been able to draw on his standard contacts into this lone wolf operation, both for security reasons and to avoid any contact with former associates who could be wired by Parnell's people after going rogue. Chief of Staff Corbett admitted the president wanted an eye kept on him even if he was operating without agency mandate. The irony was that Cody had therefore been required to "go legit," acquiring the necessary equipment: SCUBA and a "water scooter."

The tanks and respirators were easy enough to get

hold of, what with plenty of rental agencies for such devices in Maryland. Cody had his own personal dry suit, equipped with a rebreather unit that could handle the cold waters of the Atlantic. He wanted to get in and out quickly; that meant the rental of the dual motor underwater scooter with its V-shaped wing as opposed to the bullet-shaped single motor model. With the two motors, his was capable of sprints of 4.5 miles an hour. Such high speed, however, cut down battery endurance. Since he would be entering the al-Ahmad compound in a soft probe, to solve the energy demands he also carried a pair of extra batteries in his waterproof carrying case along with his clothing, his Beretta M9, and a collapsible grapnel hook.

He traveled hugging the bottom with the water scooter. Annapolis had sprawling shipping facilities in addition to its shipyards.

Shadows remained long this early in the morning, making him invisible in the Stygian depths. He was across the bay from the Chesapeake peninsula, not too far southwest of the Chesapeake Bay Bridge. He'd turned off before the mouth of the Seven River. A waterproof sleeve for his burner smart phone enabled him to keep his coordination under water, its Lexan vinyl cover allowing him to access the map on its screen.

He was required to surface a few times. There was a lot of sensitive material kept off publically accessible maps of the shoreline. The Annapolis shipyards were the source of the U.S. Navy's best and most upgraded vessels, so satellite maps and topography were placed under a very strict level of jamming and wide berthed bubbles of GPS routes.

He reached the inlet where the company's dock was situated. Angling to the dock, he located a place to secure the water scooter and his rebreathing gear. Sometime in the future, he'd come back for this equipment, confident they'd be reusable thanks to the sturdy pack in which he wrapped them. If things here went bad, if he had to make an underwater getaway, he could try for a dive down under the dock to retrieve the equipment. If Aisha was a prisoner being held on these premises, as he expected, then her extraction would have to be by land.

He scaled a ladder out of the water. No ships were docked to load or unload. Curious, but it indicated there would be little human presence about. The fewer noncombatants around—longshoremen and the like—the better. Bystanders could end up being hurt. He also intended to neutralize any security guards he encountered with a lump on the head or leave them recovering from a choke hold rather than capping some poor dude earning a buck whose only crime was guarding cargo and keeping the graffiti to a minimum.

Cody reached the top of the ladder and crouched to remove the dry suit. He folded and stuffed it into a gap. Underneath, he wore snug but warm Lincoln green jogging pants, a t-shirt and a dark purple hoodie. The subdued colors would keep him better hidden from view in the shadows, yet would not seem out of place to someone happening by on their morning jog. He tucked his sleeve-mounted phone into a side pocket of the jogging pants. The hoodie concealed his shoulder holster and the silenced M9 as well as a few other tools attached to his belt.

The dry suit would likely be discovered, if at all, by some dock worker who noticed it blocking a hole he normally flicked cigarette butts through. Yet it now was where Cody could rapidly slip the suit back on if retreat by water was required.

He moved out cautiously, watching for security patrols, observing the layout of the facility, matching it with the map in his mind. He ducked down low when he spotted a distant electric cart motoring along on its regular rounds. The two men aboard wore windbreakers and baseball caps, the unofficial uniform of security staff everywhere, and holstered sidearms. Cody maintained his stealth as he continued along, keeping to the early morning shadows.

He came upon a grouping of trailers. Three trailers long, two wide, with walkways between them, forming a contiguous perimeter inside of the chain-link fence and concertina wire. The "courtyard"formed by the trailers formed an "L" shape with a convenient parking lot for a couple of SUV's and a delivery truck.

The delivery truck was nondescript and bore the logo of a shipping company that Ahmad would be no doubt only tangentially aligned with. If the vehicle was needed, it could not later be traced back to Achmed and the force he'd brought in along with him.

The sentries wore windbreakers but the jackets were unzipped, revealing black body armor beneath the lapels. They were toting black rifles with optics and banana magazines. Cody could not determine though from this distance whether the rifles were civilian-legal arms or full military assault rifles. Either way, this was a serious upgrade in security. Security cameras mounted on posts kept an eye on the trailers. Fresh, shiny chain-link fencing surrounded the trailers. The top of the fences displayed spiraling loops of razor wire.

A shiny gloss of the metal on the perimeter fence bespoke recent installation. Big guns and extra security adjacent to the family business informed Cody that this was a temporary setup, and it would have been Achmed al-Ahmad who had it installed. It was his headquarters here in DC.

The sentries, to Cody, appeared to be South Asian Indian, both alert, their fingers off the trigger, resting on the rifles' frame. Highly trained soldiers, likely citizens of the emirates and caliphates that clung to the shores of the Persian and Oman Gulfs. Emirati Arabs were a minority in their own country but the oil money easily drew the six million Indians, Pakistanis and Bengalese immigrants who provided the manpower for the wealthy upper caste along the coasts bracketing the Strait of Hormuz.

As such, it only made sense that Achmed would arrive in America accompanied by the best of his family's trusted security force. Emirati Arabs comprised little more than eleven percent of the region's population and were not keen on doing their own grunt work . . . except for hard-driving adrenalin junkies like Achmed. According to the intel gathered by Sara and stored on the flash drive she'd left behind, Achmed had acquired quite the reputation as a jet-setting adventurer beyond having to journey about the world retrieving his wayward sister. Driving race cars, skydiving, high stakes gambling, polo . . . and all the while his robust bachelor love life entertained and scandalized the millions who followed that sort of thing in the trash media.

But Achmed al-Ahmad was anything but a glamour boy pushover. He'd come of age training alongside his father's elite military officers. Their paths had never crossed before but it was easy to flag the guy as a determined, dangerous opponent.

These sentries wouldn't be alone guarding this facility, not with the number of trailers. Those linked modular units formed a makeshift "fort" surrounded by spacious open ground. To approach, one would be easily spotted.

Cody's gaze panned the open ground, searching around in hopes of finding some way to gain entry. He rethought his jogging attire. Could he bluff his way in by pretending to be lost, an innocent civilian having wandered astray? The hoodie was large enough to conceal his gear. But he dismissed the idea. He'd come expecting a building, not a heavily guarded, concertina-wired battle station.

Scanning the dock area, he spotted a manhole cover.

There likely wouldn't be sewer tunnels beneath this point but there had to be power and gas lines for the warehouses along here. There were no electrical or phone lines visible above ground that might provide access so he utilized his smart phone, searching via the local water and power company. He wouldn't have service and internet access beneath asphalt and concrete. From the utilities schematics, he downloaded and saved the underground tunnel maps onto his phone.

Leaving the shadows and darting toward the nearby manhole cover, he reached for his grapnel hook to use as an improvised pry bar. But suddenly there came the hum of an approaching engine. He didn't automatically recognize the sound but *something* unseen—airborne!—was speeding his way. He regained the shadows at once, slipping behind stacked crates and finding cover under a pallet frame.

A remote drone!

With his phone he swept the sky, utilizing the program he'd used the night before when approaching Sara's apartment. Sure enough, the remote control device, employing its microphone, now tracked the infrasound of the drone's hover blades. Its diminutive frame, seen from between the slats of the pallet, reminded Cody of an irksome, buzzing insect.

Someone else was displaying an interest in the al-Ahmad family's business concern!

Was another party about to launch its own rescue attempt of the princess? If so . . . who? Another Vatican-based hit team? The Furies of Harmony female paramilitaries, assembled to initiate the rescue of Thelma Justice's prized pilgrim?

Cody remained out of sight, biding his time. He couldn't risk being discovered. Achmed's security force and this unknown new presence remained unaware of him. The more they concentrated on each other, the better. His every combat instinct was primed, ready to take advantage of whatever came next.

CHAPTER TWENTY-FIVE

WHEN THE DRONE swung around a building, blocking the line of sight between it and Cody, Cody burst from his place of concealment beneath the wooden slats and made a bee-line for the nearby manhole cover.

He quickly snapped open one claw of the grapnel, hooking it into the maintenance cover hatch. The improvised crowbar was an excellent substitute for the tools used by sewer and power workers to open such tunnel entrances. Using the leverage of his grapnel to lift and roll the heavy cover aside, he minimized the noise by gently lowering the lid to the pavement. Unhooking the grapnel, he closed it, reattaching it to his harness.

A line of descending rungs provided a ladder into the depths of the manhole. Cody wasted no time easing himself in and replacing the cover over him, thus doing his best to conceal his entry and presence. He climbed down. Evenly spaced small lights along the service tunnel provided adequate illumination. Pipes lined one wall. A rivulet of moisture snaked along the ground; condensation from vents at floor level.

He kept his head down and advanced. The service tunnel provided plenty of shoulder room. He jogged along. It was still early enough that he must anticipate those controlling the drone would launch their assault at any time on this complex. The rising sun would provide ample glare if they came in from the east. The pair of hard-core sentries would likely be nearing the end of their shift; fatigued, seconds slower in their response to a powerful assault.

Consulting the map on his phone in order to maintain a certainty in orientation, he made all the correct turns necessary to get him deep enough into the trailer "fortress." He slowed in his approach, matching the surface layout in his mind. He had reached another manhole rising toward a maintenance hatch close overhead.

He ascended slowly, positioning the camera of his phone against one of the pry holes in this manhole cover. The video was dim but he could discern the underside of a trailer. He estimated at least two feet of room. A tight squeeze, yeah, but he'd be inside the damn fence and, importantly, beyond sight of the sentries.

He eased up on the cover, applying slow pressure so as not to bang metal on metal, and could only grimace at the subtle grating of the manhole cover on asphalt when he edged the cover off to the side to lay it flat. The barely noticeable scraping sounded louder than that crashing freight train he'd leapt from a few days ago! Yet as he peered around from his concealment, he observed no indication of any sort of response.

So far this "soft probe" was right on track.

Even so, he drew his Beretta, slithering out of the manhole into the crawlspace beneath the trailers. Crawling on his belly. Keeping to the underside of the rectangle which made up the trailer mini-fort. While the morning light went about reclaiming the new day, long shadows remained on the west side of the courtyard, falling across the SUVs and the delivery truck, providing a modicum of cover. The encroaching sunlight made those shadows much less concealing than he'd hoped.

The windows of the trailers were curtained, offering no sign of activity. The attention of the defensive force here was focused outside of the fence.

He continued scuttling along, remaining under the pre-fab office trailers, the Beretta in his fist and pointing the way. Every breath felt like he was blowing a horn, a clarion call to summon every armed killer for miles around to come down on his neck. He made his way under a set of stairs that dropped down into the courtyard. Through the slats of the pre-fab steps, he spotted a sentry now stationed next to the big delivery truck.

Time to size things up.

Was Aisha being held in one of these trailers?

Cody didn't think so. If anyone intended to affect a rescue by breaking into the trailers, they'd be wasting precious time. Aisha was the prize possession and would be well guarded. He read their security at the front of this "trailer fort," despite the intimidating presence of the two sentries, as nothing more than a distraction; a red herring baited with skeletal security solely for appearances.

He knew from personal experience that this model of boxy delivery truck might serve as a mobile headquarters and possibly a transfer vehicle but was not particularly suitable for holding someone prisoner for twenty-four hours or more. There were little details like so-called "calls of nature," and what if Princess Aisha should try for an escape? That could raise a clamor and risk drawing attention even to this remote setting.

Still . . .

There was only one way to make sure . . . and that was to make sure.

Something was going to happen. He could sense it. But he must bide his time. There was no reason for Achmed to linger once travel plans and the woman's extraction from the States was organized. Considered in that light, if the princess was on the verge of being taken to a vessel and transported out of the country, then she very well could be temporarily confined in the rear quarters of that truck for transportation to the ship awaiting them. The windowless cargo area would easily serve that purpose for a rebellious young woman.

From his prone position, Cody could see only the empty driver's seat of the vehicle. That did not mean there wasn't a guard seated on the passenger side.

A commotion erupted from the front gate.

The sentries stationed there whipped their attention toward something approaching from the street: the third party with the drone, now making their presence forcefully known, inserting themselves into this sequence of sped-up events. Even from under that trailer at a considerable distance, Cody felt the tension of those sentries echoing the pulse in his own veins.

Now was the time to make his move.

He emerged from under the trailer and padded softly on rubber-soled boots toward the truck. His heightened combat senses amplified his every footfall to the decibel level of a stadium rock concert, while in reality the flexibility of the tough rubber tread produced less noise than a shallow breath. He moved briskly, scanning trailer windows in his peripheral vision for that one nosy set of eyes detecting his presence. But none appeared. The sentry stationed on the blind side of the vehicle went about enjoying his cigarette.

When he gained the rear of the truck, Cody launched himself into a drop and roll that took him beneath the truck's undercarriage. From there, the sentry's legs and feet were visible and within striking distance.

But things were happening at the front gate.

One of the sentries there could be heard sharply demanding, *"Halt!"* And then in an even sharper command, *"Stop where you are! This is a restricted area. Identify yourself!"*

The response to that was a chattering burst of automatic gunfire and the grille of a speeding, armored SUV slamming the front gate half off of its tracks, chain-link rattling and the steel frame warping in a powerful crash.

Cody lunged from under the truck and grabbed the sentry's ankles. The guy had naturally jerked his attention around toward the front gate. Cody flipped him onto his face swiftly and brutally. He

punched the man in the back of his head where the neck met the skull. Not a killing blow but this one would be out for a while after that impact to his central nervous system.

Cody relieved the unconscious sentry's rifle from its sling. He whirled as the passenger side door of the delivery truck swung open. A guard stumbled out, drawn by the sudden outbreak of violence. Cody reversed his captured weapon and rammed the extended folding steel stock into the man's throat. The blow toppled the guard across the truck's dash and to the floor.

A quick glance into the cargo compartment revealed a limp, bound human figure—possibly dead, possibly unconscious—tied to a chair that had been bolted to the floor. A woman's figure. Long dark hair. Tan skin. If it wasn't Aisha, it could only be a body double and what would be the sense of that? He checked the ignition of the delivery truck. Keys in the ignition. Primed to go at a moment's notice.

He gave the stunned guard from the passenger seat a stiff kick, tumbling him out of the cab. Then he slid behind the steering wheel. He had to time this right.

Even though the front gate had been smashed in by an SUV moving at a good clip, it still slowed the black truck. The guards at the gate were firing their rifles on full auto but the vehicle's dark tinted glass held. The SUV backed up. The steady stream of gunfire started producing webbed holes in its armored glass. One of the gate guards went down, ripped asunder by return fire from the SUV. The vehicle surged forward again, this time with sufficient momentum to completely heave aside the rolling gate.

A remaining sentry at the main gate burst the driver's side window with a blistering salvo. The SUV entered the courtyard only to come to an abrupt stop when it rammed into one of Achmed's parked SUV's.

Cody fired up the delivery truck's engine and stomped on the gas. The bulky vehicle snarled to life and picked up speed fast enough, heading in the direction of the main gate.

Achmed's sentry there turned, disoriented by the delivery truck springing unexpectedly to life and now coming directly at him. Before he could track his rifle around on the delivery truck, Cody ran him down with a sickening thud. A bloody crack sprouted across the lower right side of the windshield.

Once through the main gate, two more vehicles

could be seen roaring down the highway, racing side by side toward the compound. Cody steered his truck straight between the pair of them, feeling the vibration of both their fenders glancing and scraping paint off both sides of the truck that only continued accelerating away from there.

Okay!

He'd ditched a deadly crossfire, gained possession of the Princess Aisha and the "drone crew" vehicles were burning rubber, squealing around in hot pursuit.

The chase was on.

CHAPTER TWENTY-SIX

A SCREECHING metallic crash and the ugly hammering of auto fire had roused Achmed al-Ahmad from a fitful sleep.

He was in an office of the warehouse building, its window overlooking the prefabricated compound he'd ordered hastily constructed to house his team on a previous visit to the States. He regained full awareness with the gasp of a man bursting to the surface after having been submerged underwater for too long. He rolled over into a sitting position, grabbing his pistol in hand before his feet hit the floor. He'd been sleeping fully dressed in black T-shirt and jeans.

Their company ship was set to sail at noon. When they arrived at the dock, which was about thirty minutes away, last minute trickery would be involved, secretly stowing Princess Aisha aboard during the final seconds before they sailed. All was in readiness, so he'd decided to catch a rest. He told himself he must stop thinking about how every moment spent here, holding Aisha against her will, served only to give his precocious little sister more time to again slip through his fingers.

The sound of squealing tires and more gunfire rang again in his ears. He'd hurried to the window just in time to see a vehicle backing up from the gates near where the delivery truck was parked. One of his men was sprawled on the ground beside the truck, dead or unconscious. A physical struggle could be seen through the truck's windshield, and then another of his men was flung from the vehicle.

A man in dark jogging suit attire commandeered the steering wheel!

It was a surreal experience for Achmed, witnessing this unfolding firefight through the window glass like a man viewing a movie; an action movie with a frenetic pace unfolding within violent pounding heartbeats of time.

The sentries at the gate were occupied with an assault team pouring from the armored SUV that had crashed in, emptying their ammo clips at the body-armored intruders. Sentries went down amid a flurry of bullets and spraying crimson. Both sides were firing armor piercing ammunition and automatic weapons. Achmed could see the carnage wrought on the armored SUV.

He also saw the "jogger" start up the delivery truck.

The truck holding his sister raced away, storming toward the remnants of the main gate. The second gate guard got in its way. The speeding van plowed into the fellow, continuing past as it picked up speed. The sentry, dead on his feet, reeled to the ground in the van's wake.

The bulky delivery truck wheeled onto the highway where it barely missed colliding with two more arriving attack force vehicles. Then it continued speeding away while the drivers of those two vehicles executed high-speed U-turns to give chase.

Achmed aimed through the window. But if he fired, he might inadvertently kill his sister. There was still her possession of the tablet, or rather, her knowledge of it. He scooped up his radio.

"They have our package! Pick me up fast. We can't let the truck get away!"

He was already halfway to the stairs, which descended three at a time. He vaulted over the railing near the bottom step. His bare feet slapped the stairs and their knobbed, hard rubber traction bumps without effort, his feet having been toughened by the blazing hot sands of his homeland. Cushioning his jumps, flexing his knees, he had picked up his running speed when he exited at ground level.

A Dodge Charger roared to a wild stop directly before him. Ali Yusef sat behind the wheel. Another of Achmed's men, Rimat, rode shotgun; in fact, he occupied the passenger seat holding an AK-15.

Achmed leapt into the back seat at a run. The sport sedan rocketed away before he was fully inside, taking off after the delivery truck. He took a harried moment to don his shirt, coat and shoes.

"Faster, Ali. It's one lone man who has Aisha. I saw him."

"As did I," said Ali. "One man? Perhaps. But no ordinary man if he has succeeded this far."

"We *must* stop them."

Achmed detested the anxiety he heard in his own voice.

"We *will* stop them," said Ali.

He coolly steered the racing Charger through the

chaos surrounding the front gate and made it onto the highway.

Rimat said, "Sir, there's a rifle in the footwell."

Achmed withdrew the weapon. His family had money and prestige and so this was not one of the garbage rifles sold off by the millions from the old Soviet Union. It was an AK, but it had modern fiberglass replacing wood, with a folding stock, and used American military ammunition and magazines. He'd have used AR-15's for his men, but AR's didn't fold, and the AK mechanism would perform under the harshest of circumstances. Instead of rusty brown, this weapon was sleek, camouflaged with sights, an extra grip and all of the modern amenities.

He fingered the switch in his armrest that lowered the rear passenger window. He was uncertain whether his sister had been released from her restraints in the rear of the vehicle or if the jogger had simply thrown the truck into gear to immediately get her out of danger. It didn't matter. He might not have the stability of movement there in the back seat of the Charger that would allow him to score a hit to the head of whoever was driving the delivery truck. But he did have enough control to fire in the truck's general direction; four rounds that ricocheted off the pavement without flattening tires or damaging the transmission. Cody held his fire. He could not risk injuring passing motorists.

Yusef was a skilled wheelman who knew the difficulty of hot traveling at high speed through and around stopped traffic. He'd been through all manner of combat driving exercises as well as being one of the best wheelmen in Europe, having raced on the most amazing race courses, especially the infamous Nürburgring in Germany.

Rimat alerted Yusef, "We have a tail!"

Achmed turned and glanced out the rear window. A pair of saffron muzzle flashes winked back at him from a speeding SUV three car lengths behind. The rear window of the Dodge whitened where the rifle rounds struck. If there was one thing Achmed was glad for it was that he'd paid extra for bullet-resistant glass.

Firing to his rear would pose no problem. He could slow down the SUV even if only by incapacitating a vehicle in its path.

He leaned out and milked the high-tech AK's trigger. The opposing gun wagon sparked, its windshield blossoming with smears of impact on its bullet-resistant glass. He then shifted his aim and blasted the front bumper and tires of a boxy station wagon trailing the Dodge while running just ahead of the SUV.

Achmed's fire caused the wagon to swerve uncontrollably into the path of the oncoming SUV. The SUV driver did not bother to hit his brakes. The chassis of the station wagon shattered and twisted when the SUV rammed full speed into it, battering the wagon into a spin like a ballerina, stopping only when it slammed into a parked delivery van.

But another vehicle raced past it in pursuit, and another after that.

Achmed reported, "They're hot on us!"

Ali manned the steering wheel with whitened knuckles. His eyes kept shifting between looking for holes in the traffic pattern ahead and his rear view mirror.

He said, "Then we must be more nimble than their armored buckets."

Rimat lowered a cell phone from his ear.

"The police scanners are running! Local police are in motion after us."

"We need to get Aisha back," said Achmed. "If we don't catch up with that truck . . . but we *will* get her back! But these dogs behind us—"

"By Allah's will," said Ali, "This muscle car will get through this traffic!"

True to his word, the Dodge skimmed past everything in a blur as if all other traffic was frozen in place. Achmed expected to momentarily hear the crunch of metal and shattering glass as Ali cut within inches of other vehicles. Ali was blessed with a divine madness that kept their hurtling Charger from any impact that could slow them down.

The SUVs began falling further and further behind.

CHAPTER TWENTY-SEVEN

CODY KEPT the pedal to the metal.

Speeding through traffic, he was glad to see it thickening around him. The bulky delivery truck was no match for the slick, powerful, nimble automotive beast in which Achmed and his crew were chasing him. He was ahead, racing through the early dregs of traffic rolling in as Washington, D. C.'s morning commute reached its peak. He was well aware of the SUV from the mysterious third party that was also part of this chase. He could hear the rattle of an automatic weapon. Any distance he could eke out was vital in the rescue of the young woman bound in a chair in the truck's cargo area.

He eyed his inside rear view mirror to see if the girl was conscious, responsive.

"Aisha," he called into the back of the truck. "Aisha al-Ahmad! Is that you?"

Muffled noises came from within the cargo enclosure. She'd been gagged but she certainly could make enough noise.

He hoped that those giving chase behind his truck

would be infighting amongst themselves, although stray bullets would endanger civilians whose only crime was heading to work. The recovery of a princess was one thing, but this rampage occurring in the middle of a city waking up was something Cody had hoped to avoid. He could hear the smash of an SUV barreling through traffic and tearing off fenders as it blitzed along.

And there was the muscle car closing in on his ass.

Along the back track, someone was firing out the windows at the SUVs but those vehicles had to be armored at least with bulletproof glass. They were not slowed by the salvos of automatic fire. When he saw the tail end SUV of the pursuit chain slow and fall back, it occurred to Cody that there was one surefire way to deal with the tailgating muscle car in this high speed chase.

He stood on the brakes. The delivery truck's tires squealed violently as if under torture by a demon. In a heartbeat, the muscle car that had so artfully avoided intervening traffic was hitting its brakes as well. But they were traveling too fast, too close.

They inevitably collided.

The truck shuddered, the Dodge Charger hitting hard, pushing Cody's vehicle inexorably forward, the two tons of high speed muscle car striking with enough force to overcome the truck's greater weight and inertia. Cody threw the truck into reverse and pushed back once the sedan's momentum bled off. The two vehicles were entangled, the truck's full power shoving the sedan backwards into cars parked curbside. The mangled hybrid of the truck and sedan continued, crashing through a storefront. Cody figured property damage was preferable to people being run over!

He shifted the truck into Drive even as the crew in the Charger recovered enough to track their weapons at him. The truck's rear fender screamed in protest as it was torn from the truck's frame, left behind snared in the Dodge's front grille. Then a round caught one of the rear tires that blew with a bang indistinguishable from the gunfire.

Cody swerved the delivery truck around a corner, throttled at full speed. He glanced into his rear view. Aisha was wide eyed, nodding for him to keep his eye on the road. Cody did so just in time to narrowly avoid a braking city bus, thanks to her cue.

With one of the back tires shredded, control of the truck was becoming exceedingly difficult. He put all his muscle into steering the crippled vehicle. They couldn't proceed much further so Cody scanned the street ahead. He spotted a convenience store parking lot, crowded and busy at this hour, and steered sharply into the No Parking delivery area.

The truck had little enough traction with only three tires. Its front end popped upwards mounting the curb, and then came down too hard, bursting the front tires completely. The delivery truck came to a complete stop.

Cody left the driver's seat and hurried back to the bound woman. He undid her gag.

"Are you able to walk?"

Aisha screwed up her face tightly in pain.

"I am not sure. I will try."

Cody flicked open his knife and undid her wrist and ankle bindings with swift, certain slices. He helped her to her feet. She stood, but her knees were wobbly. He took Aisha's hand and the two of them left the van. Her jog was slow, but they made progress, disappearing down an alley.

An SUV could be heard zooming into the lot behind them. Cody and Aisha hobbled on.

Aisha said between heavy breaths, "Whoever you are, sir, my sincere thanks. Do we have a plan?"

Cody shook his head, no.

"Making it up as I go along," he confessed.

Intense activity from behind. The third party's SUVs were arriving. Organizational training was high on their skill set. Boots could be heard hitting the pavement. Commands shouted in Russian. A perimeter would be already established, their attention mere seconds away from penetrating the shadows of alley.

At this end of the alley, another parking lot basked in morning sunshine.

Cody selected an older, early 90's model Toyota Camry. A fully modern sedan's ignition system was different and required a complicated method to hack the CPU of the vehicle. He excelled at hotwiring older cars which had simpler electrical systems.

He took out his folding grapnel hook. He pressed one of the retractable hooks against the driver's side window. Just enough pressure forced the safety glass to disintegrate into cubes of blunted plastic. He quickly unlocked the inner door, and then hit the lock for the passenger door.

Aisha got in.

Cody went about exposing the wiring under the steering column. He stripped the wires, touched the right combination together, and fired up the car. It took a minute.

Voices from the other direction could be heard advancing closer and closer, step by step along the alley. But by the time they emerged onto the parking lot, the Toyota was gone.

CHAPTER TWENTY-EIGHT

Thelma Justice steepled her fingertips as she received the briefing from Windy regarding Jack Cody's relationship with Sara Durrell.

"Durrell is being held at Bethesda Naval Hospital under lock and key," Windy reported. "He saw her there. They communicated but no one seems to know *what* they communicated. They're coworkers but they know each other well. Durrell had an interest in Princess Aisha and that's how Cody knows about us. And we're not sure how much Durrell knows about Aisha so it gets complicated. There's a chance he's found where Aisha was taken."

"I don't doubt that," said Thelma with confidence. "You seem on edge, darling."

"I don't like it that a dangerous man like Cody is now in the mix."

"He's operating without sanction behind the back of the CIA. Technically, they can't do a damn thing on US soil." Then Thelma's eyes narrowed as she reflected further on the matter, adding, "Of course, that has never stopped them before."

"What should we do?"

"Tiff Butler has established contact with Cody."

"He's elusive and tricky," said Windy. "We won't keep a close eye on him for long unless we have a tracker placed directly on him."

Thelma shook her head.

"Too much, too soon. We'll hang back. I have access to some long range trackers. We'll keep out of range of even the most paranoid eyes and ears," Thelma said.

A phone text alert intruded.

Thelma's teeth itched at the interruption. It was Vetrov, hidden behind one of his aliases. She opened the message:

Achmed has been hit. Aisha is in the wind.

Thelma scowled.

Windy said, "Ma'am?"

She told Windy, "I asked a friend to send a search crew after the princess. But someone else has taken her from the people who had her."

"You knew where she was?"

"My friend Greb tapped his connections. He located her south of Annapolis."

"Do we know who has her now?"

Thelma did not respond to Windy's question. She was frowning, determined to remain calm, measured and composed. Thelma typed:

More information. Why did you not tell me her location?

This brought the response of a call.

She connected immediately, recognizing it as one of Vetrov's many numbers she'd been instructed never to call on her own.

Thelma answered with a terse, "This better be a secure line."

"I'm calling you on it, aren't I?"

No argument from Vetrov, simply a statement of fact.

She said, "You're careful enough."

"I have to be."

His voice, casual and yet somehow authoritative, had the effect it always had upon her, his words resonating with coarse sensuality. This turned her on while at the same time, his arrogance and his manner of command even across the telephone, were despicable male chauvinism incarnate.

"I want to trust your op security," she said. "The time has come for me to pack up and head back home. Things here in the States are getting far too dicey for comfort."

"A prudent course of action."

His condescension stung her raw nerves.

"Did you send someone in?"

"I observed from my advance team's drone."

She said, "Let's get back to what just happened. I don't mind you pursuing the Aisha matter in our shared interest. But if you had found out where she was being held and were intending to strike, why was I not told?"

"We didn't know for sure, my love. Believe me, I've been quite busy on this. We were not certain of her presence there until after the action had commenced."

"Well, if we don't have her, who does?"

"You're not going to care for this bit of news," said Vetrov. "Your interests and mine are shared perhaps even more than you thought. The drone only caught the briefest glimpse of him but my enemy, Suicide Cody, is now in possession of your princess."

"That plays," said Thelma. "Sara Durrell is in lockdown at Bethesda. I've just learned Cody has been to see her. There's our connection. I don't like this, Greb. I don't like it at all. First this Cody derails our Korean deal and now he has the princess, is that what you're telling me?"

"That does appear to be the case."

"Keep me updated."

"Certainly, my love."

She could feel his smirk across the phone connection. She ended the connection.

The safety and isolation within the impregnable walls of her chalet fortress high in the Italian Alps was calling to her stronger than ever. She had come to detest those occasions when she was forced to go out into the world of male-dominated chicanery and deceit. That would change when the planet became *her* world and with each passing day, that time was drawing near. But for now her appearance at these yearly Order of World Harmony events was important in building and strengthening the global movement of her followers; shoring up the foundations of her empire.

The present situation involving a young princess from Dubai and her ancient treasure was a perfect example. Nothing but trouble to the max at every turn. Men with guns. Sudden death everywhere. Her Furies of Harmony slain under enemy fire.

And now the one they called Suicide Cody.

CHAPTER TWENTY-NINE

SARA DURRELL WAS glad to have her hands finally free from the leather wrist restraints. She was still in this lifeless, soul-draining gray cell of a hospital room. Unblinkingly cameras watched her. Hidden microphones listened to her every breath.

They'd finally allowed her food and plastic utensils for lunch. They administered painkillers to deal with the tender flesh and battered bones which now merely ached dully, not the sharp spikes of agony that had worn her down with each blink of her eyes or movement.

"Bearable," she said.

She spoke to herself, figuring she might as well speak out loud for the curiosity of those assigned to her surveillance in this room. And it kept her from going nuts.

She spooned some vanilla pudding into her mouth and relished its light sweetness, its creamy texture as it slid off her tongue and down her throat. A guilty pleasure was an escape of sorts. Even the bland, low sodium meal had a tasty charm to it after a few days of recovery.

There came a knock at the door. It wasn't necessary; she was a prisoner and had no expectation of privacy.

The door opened. In stepped the uniformed guard who'd confronted Parnell during his recent attempt at intimidating her. She'd learned his name was Christian Bowers. He was most definitely posted to keep an eye on her and yet this soldier was not one of Parnell's hand-picked goons. He grinned at Sara with a friendly, almost boyish smile.

"What's new?"

"Nothing," Sara said with a sigh. "Nobody feels like giving me a call, mainly because they don't know I'm here."

At her request, Sara had been provided with a phone, a 70's era Princess phone featuring a twelve button keypad and all of the smartness of a goldfish.

"Too bad there's no candy match games for that old beast. At least you could keep yourself amused."

Sara returned his smile.

"Yeah. Too bad."

"Jack Cody knows you're here," said Bowers sympathetically. "But he doesn't know they've allowed you a line to the outside world, does he? By the way, word has come down that they're thinking about transferring you out of here; just placing you under house arrest instead."

That got Sara's attention. Her eyes grew serious.

"Where'd you hear that?"

"From Parnell letting off steam in front of his assistants. The guy was absolutely losing his shit."

Sara couldn't suppress a chuckle.

"Well, I have to admit that's nice to hear."

"I was three rooms over and heard every word. He's fighting it, of course. Right now I understand the guy's on his way over to Langley to plead his case. Tell you the truth, Ms. Durrell, I don't much care for that fella."

The small smile she managed was genuine and from the heart.

"Thanks, Chris, for deciding to be a friend."

The young soldier actually managed to blush with a self-conscious expression that all but said *Aw, shucks.*

There came another knock at the door.

Sara said, "Are we expecting company?"

Bowers said, "Uh, no, ma'am," but he didn't sound very convincing.

He walked to the door, routinely resting his hand on the grip of the holstered sidearm at his hip. Again Sara sensed things not seeming quite right. She leaned forward for a better look.

At the door, Bowers was suddenly and forcefully shoved backwards into the hospital room to the *crack!-crack!-crack!* of an electric stun gun firing accompanied by a bright flash. The young soldier stumbled like a drunk and dropped into a nearby chair, a dazed look on his face that was quite real.

A man strode briskly into the room. The man who'd just taken down her only friend in this building. A big man wearing the scrubs of a hospital orderly and a hospital mask. His skin appeared to be dark olive but when he got closer she could tell it was an applied cosmetic.

"Jack—"

Cody's right index finger lifted, nearly unnoticeable, to fleetingly touch his lips, directing her to silence. In his other hand, he had a couple of regular shopping bags.

Bowers had soundlessly slid from the chair onto the floor where he was on his side, curled into a fetal position, unmoving but breathing audibly.

Sara said, "Did you have to do that? He's a good young man. I like him."

"So do I," said Cody. "But it has to look good. Now hurry up."

She glanced at Bowers.

"Will he be okay?"

Cody said, in a voice barely audible even to her ears, "Don't worry. The kid's got peach fuzz but he's a pro and tough as nails, and he's smitten enough with you to jump at the chance to help."

"But you Tasered him."

"He's used to it, hon. Teaches electrical incapacitation classes and gets Tasered three or four times a month." He handed her the plastic bags. "Here. Tuck your gown into your slacks and put on these clothes. Foul this up and I'll Taser you like I did our soldier boy."

The harsh words came whispered low with affection.

Sara's peripheral vision caught movement on the floor. When she looked, she saw Bowers' hand discretely signaling her with a quick thumb's up, artfully shielded from the surveillance cameras. Fair enough.

She rose from the bed, peeling off her remaining bandages with a wince or two and depositing them into a small receptacle. Her bruises were already beginning to heal and fade. The only visible bandage she left untouched was the one covering her injured eye. Then she drew the clothes from the plastic bags. They'd been hurriedly assembled by Cody from who knew where and inelegantly stuffed into the bags. But they were her size: shoes, jeans, and a cool-weather coat. She hurriedly dressed.

"Here," said Cody.

He handed her an oversized pair of sunglass goggles

and a loose, blue knit beanie that Sara placed over her hair.

The "orderly" then loosely took hold of her wrist. Cody led Sara into the corridor. The isolation units were well off to themselves. Hospital sounds and activity could be heard from around a nearby corner of the tiled walls but at the moment, no one was in sight. They hurried to a service elevator set in the opposite wall.

Cody inserted a key, summoning a car that arrived prompt and empty. Inside and headed down, he removed his hospital mask and getup, trying to make his smile reassuring from under makeup that darkened his skin all the way to the palms of his hands.

Sara returned a smile, weak yet determined.

She said, "Jack . . ." in a quavering voice, but whatever thought she was about to speak tapered off.

This was all happening very fast. When the elevator's descent ceased, the doors again parted and Cody guided her from an obscure service side entrance, along a row of well-attended shrubbery that shielded them from view of the towering, sprawling hospital buildings and grounds. Another five minutes and they reached their destination: a decades-old Toyota compact, idling in a sun-splashed parking space on the furthest outer reaches of one of several massive parking lots.

A young Arab woman sat waiting at the Toyota's wheel.

Princess Aisha al-Ahmad!

Sara recognized her instantly though she had not set eyes on her in the flesh since that scuffle at the Thelma Justice event. This was all going down so fast, for Sara it became like a surreal dream. Was this the painkillers messing with her mind? The cool morning air seemed real enough. As did the throbbing behind her bandaged eye.

Cody opened the Toyota's rear door and helped ease Sara into the back seat, belting her in and sliding into the front passenger seat, all of this done quickly with economy of movement.

The Princess shifted the Toyota into gear.

Within moments they were gone.

CHAPTER THIRTY

THELMA JUSTICE THREW BACK another shot of vodka. The opposite wall near the main door of the hotel suite was lined with packed suitcases.

Thelma appeared contemplative, in that twilight mindset between wakeful and semi-conscious, her brain leisurely and yet thoroughly checking off each detail requiring her attention before departing the hotel within the next hour for the airport.

Tiff Butler was on her way to Paris. Windy was out and about, personally heavy-tipping the concierge staff since this hotel was their yearly regular stop for the Thelma Justice functions; monetary appreciation always kept things running smoothly in this world of high end luxury. She'd known that much even before she'd come close to attaining such status.

Now that Thelma had attained this level of financial success and independence, there was no chance in hell she was ever going back. Her media empire was secure. Thing was, the Order of World Harmony had reached a plateau over the past half-decade. This was a constant irritation to Thelma's psyche but it was all about to change thanks to a rogue Russian ex-general named Greb Vetrov, international arms dealer in diverted Russian nukes.

Thanks to the discretion and extreme personal security measures taken by both, no one in the universe would ever suspect the spiritual spokeswoman of the feminist worldview to have an overheated, almost out of control sexual affair with the kingpin Russian bad guy on the Wanted list of every major law enforcement agency on the planet.

That, in fact, was a large part of the excitement. As was the fact that the one way in which Thelma did remain unchanged from her humble beginnings was she had always loved being a slut in the bedroom! Her lesbian lovers over the years suited her but she did dearly enjoy the feel of a man's strong, coarse hands arousing her body. She loved the wicked things she and Vetrov did for each other when they were alone. Truly the world would be shocked. But no more so than if the breadth and ambition of her destiny were known.

That, of course, could never be allowed to happen. If the true intentions and plans of Thelma Justice were known, they would try to stop her.

She and Vetrov would meet again soon for more of their private fun and games. And she must get him fully committed to her vision, to her goals, and that would be in the form of the nukes he must turn over to her. That had been her plan from the very beginning of her drawing Vetrov in with her charm and her wiles. The foolish male! Vetrov thought he was conquering her as his sexual trophy. She had the man right where she wanted him. The next time they met, it would be fun and games and the next phase of her plan.

For now, though, Vetrov had worn out his welcome. He'd had his chance to reclaim Princess Aisha but he let her slip away again. Greb had texted her only a few minutes earlier. He too was breaking camp. No details but he indicated he was en route out of the country. The murder of her Furies of Harmony remained unsolved. Local police authorities assured her of their continuing investigation. But for her, this was no time to dawdle over spilt milk. Endgame. It was time to cut out. DC was getting too damn hot.

Windy let herself into the suite. Thelma could tell immediately from her assistant's expression that something had happened. Something was wrong.

Thelma said, "What is it?"

Windy cleared her throat.

"Durrell has escaped."

"Escaped," repeated Thelma. Not a question but raising the subject for discussion. She said, "Details."

"It just came in," said Windy. "The room she was being held in lost audio. Video surveillance was cut after a Middle Eastern man assaulted the soldier who was guarding her. The guard was Tased. The video is being transferred to your device."

Thelma's laptop came on. A video file popped up in her drop box. She pressed play. Thanks to the lightning connection and the top-shelf technology of the hotel and her personal devices, she was able to instantly access a multi-screen option with an individual camera, enabling view of the scene as it played out.

A man wearing nursing scrubs and mask passed into the Bethesda Naval Hospital security wing. Alone. Race? Hard to tell. Olive-hued skin. Arab? Or an artificial cosmetic applied to darken the skin? Moderately overweight. Bulky; spare tire around the middle. At first he looked fat but the illusion was dispelled when, believing himself to be unseen, the "Middle Eastern" man withdrew a flashlight-sized Taser device from under the shirt of his scrubs. The briefly lifted hem revealed his "fat" to be an array of devices, including a concealed pistol, belted about his waist!

Thelma was again wide awake, her mind and senses razor-sharp. She was estimating and calculating the passage of time during this day. Quick mental math determined that after the extraction of the Princess Aisha from her brother's clutches, a probable timeline presented itself without effort: Cody applying the disguise, prepping the right software that allowed him to penetrate the Naval Hospital's security systems.

The mask-wearing "orderly" could have been an operative of the princess's brother, Achmed. But no, force would have been Achmed's only option to gain access to Sara and question her about his sister. No, that didn't play. Thelma's screen was showing a one-man job of the "Middle Eastern orderly" gaining entry to Sara Durrell's hospital room.

Cody had disguised himself, utilizing the very nature of disease control—work clothing—and a prior visit's mental map of cameras to make it happen!

Seeing that the video was over, Windy said, "There. So you see it was a Middle Eastern that got away with Durrell. I can organize a unit of our Furies to—"

"No," said Thelma. "It's not Achmed who has her. Damn if it isn't the same mister twister who has the princess." She reversed the video, freezing it at a clearly defined head shot of the "orderly" whom she now regarded with a mixture of contempt and new respect. Thelma Justice said, "Jack fucking Cody."

CHAPTER THIRTY-ONE

CODY FINISHED SPONGING AWAY the last of his Middle Eastern skin color cosmetic.

He kept the tap running, splashing cold water onto his face, a refreshing antidote to the roadburn-like edge that was beginning to eat away at his stamina. He'd been haulin' ass and kickin' ass non-stop with only brief interruptions to offer respite. Walking and talking with Tiff Butler before that restaurant dustup. Breakfast with Corbett at the White House. And waiting on Aisha while she went into a Goodwill store to pick up clothing for Sara before the hospital extraction.

But he was running on fumes. It was time to recharge.

During the drive, Cody did pass along Barney's news concerning Greb Vetrov's involvement. She had a right to know but received the intel without comment, only the slightest nod.

Even Sara had never been to Cody's suburban safe house, a small, innocuous suburban residence in a tree-lined community inhabited by the mid-level working class of Washington. He had hopes of grabbing some sleep. The safe house was well under the radar and camouflaged behind an ownership alias no one knew anything about. He'd equipped the residence with paramilitary hardware and supplies he might need.

When they arrived at the safe house, Sara and Aisha were both showing signs of how rough things had been going for them, each holding up as best they could under an assortment of injuries. A weak but alive ember of inner strength and determination shone through the stress and exhaustion evident in Aisha's demeanor. Sara had received sufficient care and recovery time to mend from the initial trauma of her fractured orbit. Blood thinners had aided in lowering the swelling and reducing any chance of a blood clot breaking loose to cause a stroke. But it was easy enough to see that she was not functioning at one hundred percent. The safe house was stocked with more than just basic first aid, which would allow Sara to properly self-medicate if necessary.

Cody's short tour of the two-bedroom, one-and-a-half bathroom domicile ended at the safe house "supply closet." He listed off its contents.

"Medicine. Ammunition. Pick through the electronics we have and see if anything is up to date enough for secure communication. And Sara, don't take anything heavier than your finger; just examine it and leave it."

Sara, even in her somewhat disheveled condition, took mild issue with that.

"I'm not a fragile doll, Jack. You know that, right? We've taken fire together more than once."

"Never to be forgotten," said Cody. "But the orbit of your eyeball is fractured and beyond that, you have injuries that are in the process of healing. I'm just saying let's not push it. I didn't get you out of that place to lose you."

Sara nodded, wincing even from the slight head-shake. Her eyebrow stung through the painkillers.

"Okay. Point taken."

He didn't need to be reminded that Durrell was a phenomenal CIA field agent. She more often than not regretted her "promotion" out of the field to a Langley desk job. Right now, though, she was not even close to peak physical condition.

Aisha had wandered off out of earshot, curiously checking out the small, functional kitchen at the end of this hallway. Cody cupped Sara's firm chin and looked into her uninjured eye. He spoke low for her ears alone.

"Give me your take on this. Do we trust Aisha with a pistol?"

"You read my file on her? The flash drive?"

"I did."

"Considering that she's spent her life outwitting and escaping a powerful, toxic family, I'd say that young woman has more than proven her grit and moral fiber. She may be young and she may be naïve but the answer to your question is yes. Trust her. That woman is struggling to defend her independence and attain her destiny. We should help her."

Cody went through the arsenal on hand, selecting a tan-colored pistol, the upgraded version of his own trusty M-9.

He said, "Beretta M-9 A3. Smaller grip sized for her hands, and yours. Barely recoils with even the hottest ammunition. Night sights and one of the smoothest triggers and slides on the market."

Sara handled the piece, looking it over. She removed another Beretta from the gun rack for herself.

"Plus, we only need one type of magazine and ammunition."

Since Sara and the princess had already established a tenuous trust between them and since Aisha did not know who to trust—though she certainly respected what Cody had done and so she did trust him—he'd decided to let Sara take point in establishing a deeper trust and rapport with her; to impress upon Aisha that Cody and Sara were a team who had her best interests in heart and mind.

He loaded a backpack with medical supplies, magazines and 9mm rounds and then walked the pack out to the attached double garage. The Toyota would also likely be on Parnell's radar—mounted cameras covered the Bethesda parking lots—and so had been abandoned. A 2021 Ford Mustang, lined up through a connection with Barney Lund, now sat in the garage sporting fresh license plates and tools in the trunk. Cody went about preparing the Mustang. The backpack went into the trunk. The V-6 engine sitting under the car's hood had been livened up by a mechanic he knew: twin turbochargers and other engineering to pump it from 300 horsepower to a coach-team shy of 500 ponies.

A subliminal quiver prompted him to straighten and turn for a look out the windows of the garage door. Time to check for any indication that this address might be under surveillance.

What did he expect to find?

Hell, a far better question was *who* could show up. Given their number, if every faction showed up here all at once there'd be a traffic jam! He checked those factions off in his mind one by one.

Achmed al-Ahmad. Who knew what levels of resources were available to the girl's brother and his crew?

Cody could put no eventuality past them. He had a gut feeling that sooner or later he and the brother would meet on the field of conflict. Sooner would be better.

A deep cover Vatican operation. Cody could not afford to write off last night's restaurant shootout as the end of anything. They'd already killed at the Thelma Justice event. They'd be back, delivering more until they found the princess.

Greb Vetrov and Thelma Justice, whose joint resources were unlimited. The opposing team that had fought for possession of Aisha during the rescue had spoken Russian. That made for a connection between Vetrov and Justice. She was utilizing his resources. The Russian would never give up with Cody involved. It would be a personal matter for him.

The United States government. Once Jared Parnell discovered what happened at the hospital, he would command every resource available to him to apprehend Cody. A determined search, powered by the powers available to him, might locate this old counter-terrorism safe house. How long would a deep dive net thrown by agency analysts take before this site came up?

Cody muttered to himself, "Judge a man by the enemies he makes."

They couldn't stay here for long. But being on the run, with two women in tow with injuries, his options were few. They would be relentlessly hunted across the planet until Cody could find out why Parnell was so hyped to put Sara and him out of business.

He scanned the street fronting the safe house, immediately locking in on a van parked kitty corner to the safe house. No markings. No windows behind the cab, nor in the rear doors. Could be simply loaded with the working tools of some sort of contractor. But Cody's survival instincts were red flagged. A crew of workmen, wearing dark coveralls and toting large tool boxes, left the van, heading for the house before which the van was parked.

Could be a legitimate routine service call. Or it could be obfuscation and once out of sight the "workmen" could flank the safe house and attack. Cody went back into the house.

"Electronics ready?" he asked Sara.

She nodded, more gently than she had before, still wincing at the slight movement. Her Beretta rode holstered on one hip. Two spare magazines attached to her belt rode her opposite hip. She gestured with the piece of small electronic equipment in her hands, the wire of an earphone led from it to her ear.

"I'm picking up encrypted chatter close by."

"A van's parked across the street. What are they saying?"

"Can't tell. They're speaking in Russian."

"Of course. Vetrov. We know he's involved and now that he's learned I'm part of it too, he wants to finish the job that he left undone in Russia."

"You think he's one of this crew?"

"Vetrov doesn't do his own dirty work unless he's trapped in a corner and has no choice. My take is he's already somewhere else calling the shots. Where's Aisha?"

"Trolling the internet on her phone. Nothing that's happened so far today has made the news. I gave her a gun."

"How'd she handle that?"

"Her daddy built a firing range in his British mansion and probably has several more back home in Dubai. Says she's favored Berettas since she was a child."

"Range and combat are two different things."

They went to the kitchen.

Aisha looked up, setting aside her phone. Sara had outfitted the princess with a belt, holster and spare magazines.

"Mr. Cody," Aisha said in tentative greeting. "I heard you come in just now but I thought I should give you time alone with Sara." She dimpled with a shy, girlish grin. "The two of you are sweethearts. Is that not so?"

"Let's save that for another time," said Cody. "Company has arrived." He reached into his pocket and extended a ring of car keys, speaking to Sara. "Are you good to drive?"

Sara was in immediate motion, grabbing up the satchel of electronics and sliding it over her shoulder. She took the keys.

She said, "Only one way to find out."

"Get in the Mustang," he instructed, "then lay low. I have a plan. Aisha, accompany Sara. Get in the back seat of the car and stay down and out of sight. There's a blanket for you to hide under."

Aisha frowned.

"You want us to hide?"

Sara touched her forearm lightly and said, "Please, Aisha. We must work together."

"Very well," said the princess. With a small sigh, she eyed Cody. "But I must ask. What will you be doing?"

"Making life a lot harder for whoever's after us," Cody said. "Come on. Let's go. Time is running out. No more talk."

CHAPTER THIRTY-TWO

CODY WORE a modern armored load-bearing vest. A chain-mail and Kevlar shell with pocket attachments gave him access to spare magazines, grenades and other implements. In the Mustang, Aisha and Sara both had hands-free earbuds and microphones just like the ones he wore to protect his hearing as well as to stay in contact with them. A throat microphone took the vibrations of his larynx. He wouldn't even have to speak above a faint whisper in order to be heard by the women.

The enemy had their own encryption, the only way Sara could have heard them on her scanner. She'd caught the bursts of communication as the team readied to move in on the safe house.

Precautions against home invasion and preparations to defend the safe house had been made part of its general construction and design years ago. The front door was set up with a flash-bang grenade on a trip wire, mediated for those in the house by electronic ear plugs that reduced noises louder than 100 decibels to a level which wouldn't damage hearing. Cody had set the trip wire and arranged bags of boards with long nails beneath the windows, the metal points long enough to pierce through even the thickest boot sole and cause agonizing pain to anyone stabbed in the foot from stepping on them. If the boot soles had armored shanks, then stepping down on the board would cause a bent or broken ankle. Stepping into the house would draw blood or rupture ear drums at minimum, snap ankles and cause a debilitating concussion otherwise.

He'd considered lines of fire throughout the house, and located where wall panels were reinforced with steel plate would provide defense. The back door was also set with a flash-bang tripwire. The stairs up to the second floor of the house received their own trips and traps; a real world counterpart to a Christmas movie about a boy left home alone.

Now it was all about waiting, dammit. Waiting for that sound. That minor unexpected hint of movement indicating hostile intruders. Oh, they were out there all right. The tac net chatter picked up by Sara confirmed there was more than one. And they were operational.

Cody waited with his Beretta M9 pistol held in a two-fisted shooters grip. Safety off. Hammer cocked.

The front and the back doors of the residence suddenly burst open with violent explosions. A window shattered, all entry points torn apart with high explosives encased in a shell with adhesive to focus the force into one extended roar. Three entry points meant three assault teams.

A hit crew of two-man teams!

A pair of men popped into the front doorway. Cody's Beretta came up instantly. He tapped off two shots at one, then fired twice at the other. Head shots that bowled them over just as the flash-bang cut loose at 170 decibels. Blood vessels ruptured at that volume. Even wearing the noise canceling ear communication buds, Cody felt like he'd been cuffed to the back of the head. He whirled from the front door, pressing his shoulders to the living room wall, shaking his head to it from the blast he'd been prepared for.

Movement in the kitchen at the opposite end of the short hallway!

A pair of intruders were staggering about in there, stunned by the powerful flash-bang, one reeling about under the effects of the flash-bang, his partner lurching into the island in the center of the kitchen, blindly seizing the countertop with one hand unable to retain grip of his handgun which dropped to the floor.

Cody brought up the Beretta and fired. His first target's head jerked but the guy remained standing, supported by the counter. He managed to pick up his weapon.

Cody spoke a quick warning into his throat microphone.

"Sara, they're armored."

He dumped the magazine from his Beretta and switched to a fresh clip loaded with Teflon-coated bullets. He'd intended using standard fighting ammunition like hollow points in order to maximize his handgun's knockdown punch, but the armor his opponents wore made those open-mouthed bullets nothing more than ineffectual projectiles.

The gunmen in the kitchen were recovering their wits, clumsily raising weapons to track Cody. Cody commenced squeezing off rounds. The Teflon-coated bullets did their work, turning both intruders into limp bundles of discarded human life on the floor.

From behind Cody, gunfire crackled. Bullets zipped

like angry hornets, sizzling the air too damn close for comfort. He pivoted to crouch against a piece of armored wall, tugging another stun grenade from his vest. Tugging out the pin, he threw it sidearm, most of his body shielded by thick steel plate. The flash-bang struck the lead man in the doorway in the chest and exploded instantly. The blast rattled Cody's teeth.

He moved swiftly to check on a blown-out window in the dining room where he found an enemy gunman who'd come through there. The guy was on the floor, struggling to wrest a nailed board from his foot, having difficulty because the sharp nails kept him from gaining a secure grasp on the plank. He went for his pistol and triggered a fast shot, missing close enough for Cody to feel the heat of the slug as it spat past.

Cody fired. The face shield of the intruder's helmet cracked violently, high velocity tungsten puncturing bulletproof glass. The attacker shuddered violently. His hands dropped numbly. A lone rivulet of blood trickling through the bullet hole.

This one had come in alone through the dining room window. No bloody footprints led away to indicate a second intruder having entered via this route, stepping on a nail and leaving a trail of blood. Nope. This dead guy's partner was still outside.

Suddenly, the interior wall of the dining room partially evaporated, gunfire slashing through drywall. They'd placed Cody from another room by the direction of his fire. Drywall was no better than paper against this level of firepower. Steel plates had been installed up to waist level behind walls to provide the defenders unseen protection; the plates only waist-high level to allow return fire. And so Cody concentrated his return fire on the perforated wall section, his Beretta popping off round after round, expecting he was doing some kind of damage to those unseen on the other side.

He vaulted through the dining room's blown-out window, out onto the grass, landing in a shoulder roll. Sure enough, another helmeted gunman crouched outside the window, waiting for him. The guy fired, his bullet glancing off Cody's vest armor. Seeing the ineffectiveness of his bullets, the gunman bellowed Russian that could only be a curse and he charged Cody. A swift boot kick knocked the Beretta from Cody's fist.

Cody spun away from a follow-up kick, lowering during his pivot. Heel met ankle with a sharp snap. His adversary stepped away to maintain his balance, his fists balled, forearms not quite crossed to provide protection from upper body blows. Cody lunged forward and caught him in the stomach with his shoulder, the strength of Cody's folded leg giving him enough momentum and force to lift the man off his feet, throwing him backwards but somehow his opponent managed to land on his feet, digging in to arrest Cody's forward momentum.

There was no time for hand-to-hand with this Russian. Not with more intruders still inside the house who could show themselves at any second. Cody drew a knife from a sheath in his vest and with a forward lunge, he plunged the blade into his adversary's side, spearing the man in hopes of finding a gap in the body armor. Even with the blade buried ineffectually in the vest, preventing penetration, the pummeling with the blunted thrust kept the Russian off balance. He tried to grab the wrist of Cody's knife hand, bringing his knee up, a desperate kick to the balls but twist and Cody blocked the knee with his hip. Then, with the leverage of the knife blade snagged in the man's vest armor, Cody was able to forcefully maneuver the man off of his feet, intending to snap his neck with a sudden, violent crack upon the floor.

The Russian wrapped his legs around Cody's upper arm and again seized his knife arm with both hands. Cody freed his arm with one forceful tug. Planting his feet s solidly, he slammed his knee into the guy's side while delivering a punch into the bridge of flesh between the man's thighs and genitals. The guy wore a nut cup so it wasn't a debilitating, testicle crushing blow but in savage, close quarters combat, the impact was solid enough. Expelled air burst from under the helmet's visor and the claw-like fingers around Cody's forearm loosened. Cody reversed the blade, plunging it down into the man's upper chest.

Again the stab did not pierce the armored chest panel but deflected, this time sliding up the vest to drive into the gap between the man's helmet and his chest armor. Steel pierced flesh and muscle. Cody could feel the crunch of the windpipe. Bright arterial blood fountained from under the visor, Cody's knife blade planted through the roof of the man's mouth and likely in his brain as well.

Reaching down to the end of the lanyard he'd attached to his vest armor, Cody reeled in his Beretta. A figure appeared in the window just as he regained his pistol.

Gunfire and a bullet struck him in the upper torso.

CHAPTER THIRTY-THREE

The body armor saved Cody's life but the bullet delivered one hell of a punch. He grimaced, scrambling around the corner of the house to put his back to the corner wall. Checking to see if there were any barrel obstructions on the Beretta, he ejected the magazine and reloaded.

Vetrov's men weren't about to give up this effort to kill him no matter how many of them he dropped. Catching his breath, Cody muttered to himself.

"Well, at least it's better than fighting on top of a speeding train."

He pulled two smoke grenades from his heavily stocked vest, tossing one of them around the side of the house into the front yard. A dash to the rear of the house and the back yard got the same treatment, slowing Vetrov's men from rushing into those thick, billowing chemical clouds. Their collective consciousness now appreciated that he could attack them from either direction. Misdirection served the combatant as magician.

A gunman in the living room could be seen retreating from a window when he saw Cody coming at him like a shark through the ocean of smoke. Cody fired the high penetration tungsten slugs into the plate glass. The armor-piercing bullets cracked the glass enough for him to smash through the pane. He landed in a roll on the living room carpet, completing the roll in a half-seated position.

The gunman had almost made it to the dining room door. He whirled at Cody's crashing entrance. Cody shot him twice. The wounds from his so-called "cop killer" rounds would not be fatal given the guy's body armor, but two bullets to the upper torso did drop him.

Bullets slashed at Cody from the front hallway.

A reflexive scramble sent him from the living room, across the dining room's hardwood floor, triggering off rounds but whoever had fired on him from there could already be heard hustling down the hallway that bisected the house.

He said to Sara across the two-way, "Trouble coming your way. He's wearing armor."

"We're ready," came Sara's prompt response. "Those armored cups still leave thighs and knees vulnerable."

Cody could not help but grunt a grin across the connection.

"Give 'em hell, babe."

Sara would be using the Mustang's automatic window. The mechanism was quiet, barely audible. Yeah, he had faith in Sara's abilities as a seasoned urban warrior. She'd proven that she was sudden death in a fire fight. Soon as these intruders were dealt with, he'd be behind the steering wheel of that Mustang and tearing the hell out of here!

His mental timer ran the numbers. Either his opponent would come around the corner of that archway from the living room or not. He rose to a knee, eyeballing the hallway and moving with a soft step.

An object clunked on the hardwood floor behind him. A flash-bang grenade, identical to the ones he'd placed against these guys.

He screwed his eyes shut and let loose with a full-throated shout intended to equalize the pressure in his ears when the flash-bang went off, making the deafening, brutal blast only one-tenth as painful to his hearing. The shock wave of the grenade's detonation slapped him across the face with all the gentleness of an18-wheeler skidding with no brakes. Even through his clenched eyes, 12 million lumens produced by the flash powder in the explosive turned the insides of his eyelids bright yellow. An after-image seared his blurred vision. The ear buds he wore were good but 170 decibels was sufficient sonic pressure to possibly induce permanent deafness.

Somewhere in the distance, behind the blast's wall of rumbling thunder . . . *a gunshot cracked!*

He lurched behind a dinette and hutch as more bullets sniped the air. Compared to the miniature sun which had just burned his retinas through clenched eyelids, the muzzle blast of a handgun was negligible, a mere flicker of gunfire but it pinpointed the enemy's position for him. He aimed and fired, aiming behind where the muzzle flashes appeared. One of his armor-piercing bullets clanged loud enough to register in his battered hearing; he'd aimed low, his round striking one of the steel plate reinforcements embedded in the walls.

The hutch shuddered, bullets slamming into its wooden sides; sliding glass doors and old china set on its shelves shattered under the barbaric assault. Cody felt a bullet strike his armor, searing a furrow in the skin over his triceps. Shallow but it burned like hell; a flesh wound. The muscles in his arm muscles avoided damage but he felt the armor also taking dull punches to his chest and side. He rolled into the open. His opponent had stepped into the archway and now spun in his direction, responding to his sudden movement. The Beretta spat a 9mm slug that jerked the man violently, Teflon coated death drilling through his SWAT helmet and body armor.

Cody murmured to himself, "One more to go."

The last of the intruders could be heard shuffling along the hallway from the garage.

Cody stalked forward to intercept the guy who was limping. The door behind him, which connected the house with the garage, remained ajar. Through it, Cody saw that the Mustang had taken fire. Smears of bare metal were visible where bullets had scoured the paint job. But the marred steel was intact. The man's limp said the ladies in the garage had given as good as they'd got.

The guy was shuffling along lost in a world of pain from whatever wound he'd sustained. He drew up when confronted by Cody, who wanted to take this one alive if he could. He might be able to reveal Vetrov's present location. But the injured intruder stunned Cody with the speed and force of his reaction. He tried pistol whipping Cody.

The hard metal of his pistol barrel ground along the side of his jaw sent Cody stumbling against the bullet-riddled wall, his Beretta dropping to the floor. The intruder fired and if Cody hadn't dipped his head, the bullet would have scooped out a divot of his skull. Cody punched the guy's forearm, sharp and hard. A second bullet lodged in the ceiling. A follow-up punch to the man's biceps jarred the guy's pistol from numbed fingers.

It was now bare knuckle fighting and Cody, even in his winded condition, remained hopeful of taking this one alive.

The man whipped his helmeted forehead forward for a head butt. Cody barely lurched out of the way in time, taking the helmet blow to his shoulder. Had the head butt landed as intended, Cody would have been dealing with a concussion of his own or a skull fracture. He wrapped his arm around the man's neck, effectively immobilizing the both of them. Rapid punches landed on Cody's stomach and his sides, hardly noticeable after having taken bullets to his body armor at those same body locations. He twisted.

They staggered around in a circle in each other's grasp. His enemy's steel-toed boot delivered a swift kick to Cody's knee, igniting fire erupting in his shin, knocking him off balance. The two men spiraled into a sprawl on the floor and crashed hard together. The assassin wrenched free from Cody's grasp and his sledge-hammer fist swung down. Cody's forearm blocked the punch. Cody could only block his opponent's helmet and body armor making any punch he threw ineffectual. The armor-clad leapt to his knees ready to continue fighting.

That's when Sara Durrell stepped into view, a two handed grip on the Beretta that she tracked on the guy but not fast enough. He wheeled in her direction and lunged, seizing her wrists in his powerful hands.

Behind him, Cody had made it to one knee, his head swimming.

Thirty hours without sleep. The flash-bangs. The fist fights. The high intensity pounding of adrenaline. Bullets to his armored torso. All of it bordering a floating haze of numbness. Once the guy wrestled the gun from Sara, it would all be over.

And Sara was already beginning to lose the struggle . . .

CHAPTER THIRTY-FOUR

CODY LEVERAGED himself against the floor with his hands, drawing his knees to his chest. He thrust himself to his feet. His arms felt heavier than lead, his torso painful in a dozen spots. Planting his feet on the floor, he launched himself at where Sara was wrestling with the heavily armored man for control of her Beretta, her face grimacing in what must have been blinding pain. Yeah, the past thirty hours had taken its toll but he managed in the leap to encircle his arms around the neck of Sara's assailant.

The guy lurched back against Cody but checked the involuntary movement, managing to retain his balance. His helmeted chin was jammed into Cody's elbow. Cody slammed his knee into the back of the thigh. A wail of pain escaped from under the helmet. The knee must have caught his opponent in whatever wound he'd sustained in the garage. His legs buckled. Cody brought even more of his weight on the man's neck while Sara struggled to hang onto the handgun. She kicked the guy in his wound, causing him to jolt wildly while locked in Cody's constricting grasp.

Cody tried to sink his fingers under the man's visor, to peel the helmet off of his opponent, to provide something other than a single gunshot wound in the leg as a weak point. The man rammed a poly-carbonate shielded elbow into Cody's groin, a brutal blow he felt even through his jock cup. The edges of the protective shell stabbed into sensitive flesh. Cody winced. With only the choke hold under the man's chin, he didn't have leverage enough to snap the guy's neck and the armored face plate didn't allow enough room to strangle the throat.

The intruder punched Sara between her legs, weakening her knees. She dropped to a kneeling position but continued forcefully fighting to keep her hold on the Beretta. Cody was regaining possession of his pistol, tugging at the end of its lanyard. His opponent took advantage of the loosening of Cody's death grip to apply additional strength in his continuing effort to rip the pistol from Sara's grip. To counter this, Cody forced the man's chin up, simultaneously drawing his pistol another foot closer. But then a hard-shelled elbow cracked down on his forearm reaching for the gun, arresting that effort.

It was a stalemate. If Cody could regain his pistol, with the few armor-piercing rounds remaining in its magazine, he could fire through the Kevlar that protected the man's vital organs. If his opponent got control of Sara's Beretta, she and Cody would be vulnerable. So Cody forgot about working his Beretta's lanyard. He snaked his arm to trap the intruder's limb when the guy jerked his elbow back to deliver another blow to Sara. This left the man only one hand free to fight Sara for control of her gun while Cody continued stretching and craning the guy's chin up and back, thus making the throat more vulnerable. The man's grasp was starting to slip from around the barrel of the pistol he and Sara were fighting over.

Cody twisted and stretched his opponent's trapped upper arm. He could hear the pop of tendons. The man finally released his grip on Sara's pistol, instead slashing down on her wrist with a lightning speed karate chop that caused Sara to drop the Beretta. The gun clattered to the floor, skittering away. Their opponent threw another punch at Sara, narrowly missing her injured eye. She dodged a follow-up swing, and then dove in close.

"Get the gun!" Cody growled.

As the three of them fought, struggling to and fro in a weird, violent dance, Cody could feel a tugging against his holster. But with both arms engaging his foe, he could not tell what was happening. The man's fingers where clawing desperately at Cody's choking forearm, trying to break Cody's crushing hold.

A pistol barked.

The man jerked violently in Cody's grip.

The gun snapped again.

A shell casing bounced off Cody's wrist. The man sagged in his grasp. The two of them tottered back and forth.

Sara stepped in to help Cody disentangle from the dead man. She still held his Beretta, its front sight and barrel ensnared in the armpit of the guy's body armor. The black lanyard cord trailed from the pistol back to his holster. They let the body drop to the floor like a sack of old dirty clothes.

Cody said, "Thanks, hon."

"Payment for busting me out of stir," said Sara with a small smile showing through the pained discomfort of her weakened condition.

The Mustang's horn sounded from the garage.

They found Aisha leaning over from the backseat, working the horn to get their attention. She'd followed orders and remained where Cody had requested but now her expression glowed with the urge to be gone.

"Come on!"

They had started toward the car.

One of the garage doors suddenly shook mightily with a loud, slamming impact.

At first it sounded loud enough to be the detonation of another flash-bang grenade!

Cody dumped the empty clip from his Beretta, feeding it a fresh box of copper-jacketed slugs. He and Sara glanced through the window of the two-car garage.

The front grill of an SUV had rammed full speed into one of the doors, busting it inward. The door was twisted off of its hinges, half-toppled from its runners. The SUV backed up, materials of the door frame twisted in its bumper. The driver stopped, shifting for another run to finish the job.

A gunman on the passenger side leaned out his window. No helmet shielded this one's face. He wore a black windbreaker, a stubby assault rifle in his hands. Cody took aim and fired. The rifleman slammed back inside the truck cab, and then slid down out of sight beneath windshield level.

"Talk about thorough," grunted Cody.

"An entire hit team," Sara nodded, "*and* they have backup!"

Cody snapped more rounds at the van's windshield. Instead of bullet holes, a line of white smears of flexed bulletproof glass appeared. The driver poked his left hand out his window, a pistol in that hand. Bullets spanked the wall behind and above Cody from the wild shots. Powdered drywall spat clouds of chalky dust into the air. Cody fired at the driver's arm. The guy dropped his handgun, a bloodied forearm dripping blood.

"No more mister nice guy," Cody grumbled.

He snagged a grenade from the armored vest. Unlike the smoke and flash-bang grenades, this was a high explosive anti-personnel number. Chawing the pin free with gritted teeth, he rolled the egg-shaped grenade like a miniature bowling ball.

It traveled where he aimed it: beneath the carriage of the SUV.

The grenade detonated with a ferocious blast, high velocity fragments launched at thousands of feet per second. The façade and front walkway of the safe house took shrapnel but the undercarriage of the SUV absorbed most of the blast, a raw shock wave of wicked force that blew out the vehicle's front wheels, snapping the axle in half. Floorboards of the SUV must not have been armored; a gust of pink misted out both windows of the cab.

A rear door opened. A ragged, charred, stumbling human figure, holding a gun, took several steps from the ravaged truck. Cody braced, ready for even more conflict. But the guy collapsed into a pile of humanity that looked more like a pile of ashes. Cody fired a single mercy shot, then turned to enter the garage.

He and Sara threw themselves into the Mustang. Cody took the steering wheel. Sara sat next to him in front. Aisha leaned forward between them from in back, her expression aglow alive more with excitement than fear.

Cody didn't even bother with the garage door remote. The front bumper of the Mustang was reinforced just like its doors and bulletproof windows. The muscle car burst through the second garage door like a lion leaping through a paper hoop at the circus. Tires caught hold on street pavement with a shrieking squeal and they were on their way.

"Where are we going?" Aisha called, her adrenaline channeled into pure enthusiasm.

Sara gripped the dashboard with both hands.

She said, "Uh-oh."

She'd spotted what already had Cody tapping the brakes, slowing the Mustang.

Slowing, but not to a stop . . .

Ahead, in the middle of the residential street just short of the next intersection, a pair of unmarked white, windowless vans was traveling in their direction. When the Mustang was spotted from about a quarter mile distance, the second of the approaching vans drew into the oncoming lane. Both these vehicles came to a stone stop in the middle of the street, the vans parked nose to nose, effectively blocking the sun-splashed street.

Before these vans came to a complete stop its occupants—five from each—poured onto the street: women in khaki paramilitary uniforms, armed with automatic rifles. With well-trained precision they established a line across the width of the street, standing shoulder to shoulder with their weapons held at port arms.

"The Furies of Harmony!" Aisha exclaimed.

Sara told Cody, "They're Thelma Justice's security force."

Aisha was practically bouncing in her seat with giddiness.

"They've come to rescue me!"

Cody held the Mustang at a crawl, scoping out the situation ahead with narrowed eyes.

"Looks more like a hijack then a rescue."

"But I came all the way here to see Thelma Justice," said Aisha. "I don't understand. What are we . . . what are *you* going to do?"

Sara studied the man behind the wheel. The man she knew so well. She buckled her seatbelt.

She said, "Aisha, buckle yourself in and stay down."

The princess did as she was told, frowning with uncertainty.

"What's going on? Aren't you going to stop for them!?"

One of the Furies fired a single shot. The high-powered report echoed loudly in the open street. A bullet failed to penetrate the Mustang's bulletproof windshield.

Aisha shrieked.

Sara said under her breath, "Oh, hell."

Cody said, "No, we're not stopping. Not after what we've just gone through. We'll sort it out later. But no one's stopping us and I've killed enough people for one day. Hang on, ladies."

He booted the Mustang's accelerator to the floor.

CHAPTER THIRTY-FIVE

THE MUSCLE CAR goosed into high speed instantly with an upshift and a squeal of tires, leaving in its wake a white cloud smelling of burnt rubber.

That line of Furies of Harmony may have had professional training and discipline but they scattered fast soon as it became apparent that the warning shot was going unheeded. It's one thing to appear menacing behind the barrel of a gun. Quite another to put one's life on the line face-to-face with the oncoming grille of a high speed automobile!

The Mustang's reinforced grille and chassis plowed through the barricade of nose-to-nose parked vans, a hell of a jarring smash as the Mustang continued gaining speed, knocking those empty vehicles aside as if they were discarded bowling pins. A handful of shots rang out from behind without effect even when rounds spanged off the Mustang's tail end. Cody took the nearest corner on two wheels and a prayer, accompanied by more squealing of tires tortured across pavement and another burnt rubber cloud befouling the sunny air.

No one behind them had regrouped fast enough to follow.

Cody dropped the Mustang's speed down to just under the legal limit. He linked onto a freeway, then pulled off two exits later to travel residential streets to determine if anyone somehow had managed to pick up their scent.

Twenty minutes of this within the confines of the Mustang seemed to drag on longer because of the tension among its occupants. Cody was on edge, damn straight, though he remained keenly aware of everything around them, closely watching his rearview mirrors. And yes, he knew Sara well enough from previous high stress situations to know she remained an asset. Aisha, on the other hand, had lapsed into a sullen, uncommunicative silence, trolling on her smart phone.

When he felt confident that they were free and clear of what had gone down in and around that very *un*safe safe house, Cody pulled over and quickly changed license plates on the Mustang. Then they rejoined the freeway traffic flow which was busy as usual though at least it was between rush hours. At one point a blur of speeding police vehicles, lights and sirens wide open, raced past them going in the opposite direction, no doubt responding to a radio summons response to the unleashed warfare in suburbia.

Sara kept searching across the full dial band on the car radio but without results. For the time being, the authorities were obviously keeping a news lid on the shootout; SOP in today's dangerous world of urban mass shootings.

Cody said over his shoulder, "Aisha, any news online?"

The princess hadn't quite processed everything that

was happening. She did not lift her eyes from the phone screen.

"Nothing," she said simply.

Cody didn't blame the young woman for that, not one bit. There was plenty to process for damn sure. And he was not exempt. Greb Vetrov was obviously the one responsible for the kill crew that had initially assaulted the safe house. But then there was the follow-up confrontation with the Furies of Harmony. In his inventory before the battle of the forces aligned against him, he now realized that he'd neglected to include Thelma Justice on the list.

As if reading his mind, Sara looked up from scanning the radio dial.

She said, "What do you make of those Furies of Harmony showing up? They were backing up the Russians."

"I don't think so," Cody countered. "If it happened that way, it would have been better coordinated. Those Furies showed up representing no one but themselves. They were just late showing up to the party."

"But how did they know where to show up? How did they know the princess is with us?"

"Make a guess."

"An alliance between Thelma Justice and your nuke-dealing Russian? Thelma got her information from Vetrov?"

The princess, overhearing this, leaned forward from the back seat. Her expression, reflected in Cody's inside rearview mirror, was a mask of uncertain emotion.

"But you cannot be serious, these things you say! Ms. Justice would never consort with heartless killers and kidnappers! Her entire life is devoted to spreading the healing power of tolerance and love. It is why I came to America to meet her."

"Let's talk about that," said Cody. "People have died over the past few days over an artifact said to be in your possession."

"At first I considered bringing it with me here to America. But I was not sure who to trust and so I made other arrangements."

Sara said with a frown, "You mean it's not even here in the States with you?"

"Yes, that is what I am telling you."

Cody said, "Tell us about this artifact."

Aisha squirmed under his attention. They were all running on empty. Aisha's shoulders sagged.

"It is the key to my family's wealth, you see. An ancient treasure from the time of the Crusades, locked away in a hidden fortress."

Sara said, "I researched your family's background. It's not generally known but they did not make their money in oil. But Aisha, are you suggesting the Vatican sent killers after Cody because of buried loot from the Crusades?"

Without hesitation, Aisha nodded.

"More than that! The legend of the Knights of the Temple is well known; how they were betrayed by the Vatican. That's the *known* legend. The Knights and their families, their women and children, were slain in a brutal ambush on Friday the 13th,1307. And yes, all over treasure taken from the Holy Land, or so it is said."

"Here's the question that has intrigued me from the beginning," said Sara. "Why should any of that interest Thelma Justice and The Order of World Harmony? She certainly has more than enough money to have little need for an ancient buried treasure."

"It is explained by what is *not* so well known," said Aisha. "You see, my family knows the truth that the Pope and all of his predecessors before him do not want spread unto the world. Many of those knights were women! Priestesses! Ancient documents and artifacts handed down into my family's possession verify this. Implicit is an even older item that was in possession of the knights; an admonition by God regarding the holiness of *all* His creation, pointing toward the equality of women and men in religious practice. This of course radically challenges the traditional view of faith and gender. Do you not see? Such from God would greatly inspire manifesting the goals of The Order. I wanted to give the artifact to Thelma Justice once I established a friendship or at least an association with her integrity. But now . . . everything has me confused, I must say."

Cody saw the numbers adding up behind Sara's eyes even through the painkillers and her splitting headache.

Sara said, "A new brand of global feminism inspired by the Knights of the Temple? It does have the ring of plausibility."

Cody said, "Where is this relic?"

"I sent it to Russia," said Aisha. "Mailed it book rate so nobody would give it a second glance. It's waiting for me in a post office box I set up when I was on holiday in Moscow six months ago. The post office in the Beletoz Building."

"Beletoz," Sara repeated thoughtfully. "That's familiar."

She pulled out her tablet and began scrolling.

"Beletoz is a Russian mafia front," said Cody. "I researched them when I was hunting Vetrov. Couldn't find much."

Sara looked up from reading her tablet screen.

"The Beletoz building also has corporate offices rented by Thelma Justice."

Cody frowned.

"Thelma and Greb Vetrov are crossing paths too damn often."

"No!" said Aisha. "I cannot believe Ms. Justice would be involved with such people. I want to trust you both, I really do. But . . . I don't know what to think or who to trust!"

Cody took a deep breath, exhaled it slowly.

"I know the feeling, Princess, believe me. And you need to know this: at any point, Sara and I will allow you your freedom. I'll take the next exit and pull over to let you out at the curb if that's what you want."

"I'm not sure what I want," said Aisha, "but I know what I *don't* want that." Her gaze acknowledged the bullet hole in the windshield. "I am in danger but I am used to that. There are always, it seems, those who would hurt me, even my brother Achmed, who has my family's resources at his disposal. He will stop at nothing. But you two have risked your lives for me. You both have earned my undying trust, yes. But with everything that is happening . . . Mister Cody, what are you going to do next?"

Sara eyed the man behind the steering wheel.

"Y'know, Cody, I was wondering that same thing myself. I, uh, do hope we're not on Suicide Cody's last mission."

"Not hardly," growled Cody. "They might have stuck me with a name but that's not what it's about anymore."

"I'm very glad to hear that," said Sara with visible relief.

"We've got an ex-Soviet general wholesaling nukes," said Cody, "and he hooks up with someone who wants to initiate a new world order. That's a bad mix. Okay? That's a long way from a burnt-out case, me, wanting to check out. I want to take down the ones who push people too far. The bullies. The exploiters. The fear mongers."

"The bad guys," said Sara. "And let's not forget the little matter of why the hell is Jared Parnell so gung ho hell-bent on taking us out of the picture. You know I'm in on this, Cody. All the way and to the limit."

"Good to know," said Cody. "How about you, Princess? It's decision time. We're going vigilante, Sara and me. We're going to track this trail wherever it takes us and then where going to shake their cage, whatever it is they're up to. Are you in or out?"

Sara added, "Things will get rough but if you stay with us, we'll do our best to keep you alive."

The trace of an impish smile touched Aisha's lovely features. Her dark eyes sparkled with an inner strength and determination.

"That is reassuring. I accept your offer and will accompany you," she said somewhat properly. "The trail will lead us to the truth. And since you have armed me, for my part I will do my best to preserve your lives as well."

Sara's eyes remained on Cody.

"Which leaves only one question remaining at this point: what's our next stop? Where are we going?"

"We're on our way to the airport," said Cody, "and we've got calls to make before we get there." He thought of Barney Lund. "I've got a buddy who can help ease us out of the country and I'm willing to bet that between us, we've got a few friends left in the CIA who will lend an undercover hand if we ask. The only place to pick up Vetrov's trail is the same place Thelma Justice has an office and the princess has a priceless book rate package waiting in a post office box."

"Sounds easy enough," said Sara, reaching for her smart phone.

"It will be dangerous," said the princess, "but if anyone can do it, *we* will succeed no matter what forces are summoned against us."

"Glad you agree," said Cody. "Next stop: Moscow."

A LOOK AT BOOK TWO:
LETHAL ASSAULT

A Match Made in Hell!

Cody's missions as top American agent, "the President's man," have seen him tackle terrorists, drug lords and international assassins. But nothing—*nothing*—could prepare him for the potent alliance of evil created when General Greb Vetrov teamed up with Thelma Justice.

Vetrov is *the* global arms dealer, specializing in the sale of diverted Soviet-era Russian nukes to terrorist groups and rogue nations. One of the wealthiest criminals alive, no photograph of Vetrov has appeared in years. He's a noted ex-military strategist who literally wrote the book on prevailing nuclear endgame theory. Thelma Justice is the biggest media star since Oprah. Her wealth, influence and global media presence is unrivaled. The insane obsession secretly shared by these two: decimate civilization with Vetrov's nukes so Thelma's "enlightened" worldview can rise from the ashes with her as its ruler.

For Suicide Cody and Sara Durrell, it's a red-hot race against time to stop this New Millennium Bonnie and Clyde from blowing up the world. And time is running out . . .

"Stephen Mertz is a Grandmaster of action/adventure novels!" — MensAdventureMagazine&Books.com

AVAILABLE APRIL 2022

ABOUT THE AUTHOR

Stephen Mertz is an American fiction author who is best known for his mainstream thrillers and novels of suspense. His work covers a wide variety of styles from paranormal dark suspense (*Night Wind* and *Devil Creek*) to historical speculative thrillers (*Blood Red Sun*) and hardboiled noir (*Fade to Tomorrow*). Mertz is also a popular lecturer on the craft of writing and has appeared as a guest speaker before writer's groups and at universities.

During high school and college, Steve regularly scandalized his "literary, well-intentioned" creative writing teachers with "thud and blunder melodramas." Throughout military service, travel, and a wide variety of jobs, his goal remained to become a publishing, full-time freelance professional. "It was never a question for me of if, but always when." His first national sale was to a mystery magazine, and his first novel, a detective thriller entitled *Some Die Hard*, was published under the pseudonym of Stephen Brett. Another Brett novel followed, as did a string of mystery and suspense short stories.

Steve's writing output increased dramatically when he emerged as one of the country's most in-demand writers of adventure paperback novels, averaging four books per year for ten years. His work on Don Pendleton's Mack Bolan series is regarded by fans as some of the best in that series. He also created the Mark Stone:

MIA Hunter and Cody's Army series, written under the pseudonyms Jack Buchanan and Jim Case respectively.

Stephen Mertz has traveled widely and is a U.S. Army veteran. He presently lives in the American Southwest, and he is always at work on a new book.

Printed in Great Britain
by Amazon